THE
LAKE

A BERRY SPRINGS NOVEL

AMANDA
MCKINNEY

Paperback ISBN

978-0-9989599-5-5

eBook ISBN

978-0-9989599-3-1

978-0-9989599-4-8

Credits

Editor: Teri Anne Conrad

ALSO BY AMANDA MCKINNEY

And many more to come...

For Mama

PROLOGUE

HER HEART RACED as she stared out the dirty, smudged window. The full moon that lit the sky earlier was now blanketed by thick cloud cover. The late night was as black as coal and the temperature had dropped at least twenty degrees in the last hour. A storm was brewing. It was about to break loose.

She shivered as a gust of wind blew in through the open window. The metallic taste of blood seeped into her mouth where the gag had rubbed the corner of her lips raw. Her wrists burned from the zip ties. Where the hell were they taking her?

Wide-eyed and riddled with nerves, she glanced over at the driver, and then at the passenger. Not a word had been uttered since they'd kidnapped her from the parking lot. Not a single word.

She anxiously looked ahead, but could only see as far as the dim headlights would allow. The driver gripped the wheel with both hands, his knuckles as white as his face as he barreled down the old country dirt road.

Where the hell were they going?

She should have listened to her parents and never gone out for a jog past dusk. She should be at home, asleep in bed like most seventeen year olds. Dammit, she should have listened to her parents more often. She prayed she would have another chance to listen to them.

Lightning slashed the sky as tiny raindrops began to speckle the windshield. Her body jolted as thunder crashed above them. The musty, moldy scent of lakeshore filled her nose.

Finally, the car began to slow. Directly ahead, she saw a dilapidated dock, extending out into the water, and a small fishing boat tied to the side. The churning, angry lake was almost invisible in the dark night.

The car rolled to a stop and the engine cut off.

No one moved.

No one said anything.

Until…

"Make the call." The passenger looked at the driver.

The driver nodded, pushed out of the door and walked to the front of the car; his body outlined by the headlights.

Her heart thudded wildly in her chest and despite the chill in the air, sweat beaded on her forehead. Who were they calling? What the hell did they want with her?

She looked at the passenger, who was staring straight ahead. Calm, cool and collected.

After a moment, the driver lowered the cell phone, turned and looked at the passenger through the windshield. His beady eyes narrowed and he shook his head, and something in her stomach churned.

And then, his gaze cut to her.

Her pulse spiked.

The passenger nodded and stepped out of the vehicle as the driver walked around and opened the back door. He leaned in and said, "Get out."

Hot tears began to fill her eyes.

"I said, get out."

Her legs felt frozen, her body stuck to the car seat.

"*Get out!*"

He reached in, grabbed her arm, and yanked her out the door. Her body fell like dead weight on the wet, muddy earth beneath her. Droplets of cold rain began to slick her hot skin. Her chest felt heavy, her whole body locked with fear. She took a deep breath.

Inhale, exhale, inhale, exhale.

Lightning lit the sky, followed by thunder. The rain began to pick up.

The front door slammed, echoing through the night, and the passenger looked down at her with an expression as cold as ice.

"Grab the cinder block and more rope."

No. No, this can't be happening. Oh, my God, this can't be happening.

The driver opened the trunk and retrieved a small bag and a block.

"Get up, let's go."

He pulled her to a stance, and shoved her forward.

Her legs felt like lead as she walked down the path, her shoes sinking in the mud with each step. Rain poured down her face.

Please, please wake up from this nightmare.

The dock creaked and swayed as they stepped onto it.

"Get in the boat."

Thunder boomed as she clumsily stepped into the boat as it was untied from the dock.

"Sit."

Her mind raced. This was going to be it; the end of her life. She had to get out of this boat. She had to do something. She had to get away. *Now.*

Like a flash of lightning, she spun on her heel and lunged toward the dock. The moment her foot hit the wood, a hot pain seared her side.

Fuck!

Pain shot through her and she felt warm blood trickle down her skin. She'd been stabbed.

"*Dammit*, why the hell don't you listen?" The man yanked her backward and threw her on the boat floor. As she writhed in pain, the passenger grabbed a rope from the bag and began to tie it around her ankles.

Tears ran down her face. Any hope that she had was gone. This was it. She was going to die.

Through the gag she begged, "Please. Please don't do this. Please, I won't turn you in; I'll never go to the police. Please just take me home."

The engine roared and smoke puffed out the back, clouding the passenger's face.

"We need to hurry."

Lightning slashed the sky as the boat jolted forward and picked up speed. The rain felt like knives pelting against her skin. The cold wind whipped through her hair and her whole body shivered in response.

Finally, they reached the middle of the lake.

The boat stopped, and the engine cut off. Dread for what was about to happen next paralyzed her.

"Where's the cinder block?"

Her body seized with terror as the cinder block was tied to the rope that was tied to her feet.

The passenger gave instructions. "You get the feet, I'll get the head."

Oh, my God, no.

She screamed until her tonsils felt like they were going to burst as she was lifted in the air. She looked up at the dark sky, her eyes mad with panic as rain poured down her face.

"One..." she was swayed back and forth, "two... three!"

Her body went weightless in the air as she was thrown from the side of the boat.

A bolt of lightning, like a witch's hand, pierced the sky.

Her body hit the water, the cinder block splashing a moment later.

The water spilled over her face as she looked up at her captors, before being dragged down into the darkness.

CHAPTER 1

THE DOOR SLAMMED behind her as she took one last glance over her shoulder. Only the flickering neon light of *Dave's Bar* cut through the dark night.

Frequented mainly by truckers, cowboys, and drifters, Dave's Bar was surrounded by thick woods and endless dirt roads. The closest building was Smarty's Gas Station, ten miles west.

It was a perfect meeting place.

Jolene shook her head and zipped up her black, leather jacket as the cool October wind whipped through her long, dark hair.

She should have known. She'd never liked Chase, never trusted him. But it wasn't until after they'd begun working together that she realized what a snake he really was. And dumb. Dumb as a box of rocks, and ignorance was the one thing Jolene did not tolerate. Well, that and someone trying to stiff her out of her cut which he had just tried to do. Emphasis on *tried*.

She grinned. Maybe she shouldn't have broken his wrist, but the little rat had to learn somehow.

The low moan of old country music whispered through the air as she walked to her car. Dead leaves danced across her boots as she reached into her pocket and pulled out two envelopes from behind her Glock 9mm. The one that she was supposed to give to him, and the one that he was supposed to give to her. Just as she suspected, the one intended for her was empty. She rolled her eyes and shook her head again. What a bastard. She crumpled the empty envelope and tossed it in the bed of a nearby truck.

Jerk.

She then opened the other envelope, and fingered the hundred dollar bills. At least the night wasn't a total loss.

As she reached into her purse for her keys, the front door burst open. Before she could turn her head, his footsteps pounded the gravel behind her.

Shit.

Searching for her keys, her fingers scrambled through her purse but there was no time. For a fleeting moment, she considered her gun, but she didn't want to go down that road.

Run.

She turned on her heel, sliding on the gravel before taking off in a sprint.

She slung her purse across her body and darted through the gravel parking lot; his heavy footsteps close behind her.

Up ahead was a barbed wire fence and the tree line just beyond that. She sucked in a breath, pushed to a full sprint and scaled the fence by barely an inch.

So did he.

Her heart hammered in her chest as she burst into the woods. The moonless night darkened the woods as black as ink as she squinted to see ahead, or anything at all. Twigs and branches slapped against her face, the thick brush threatening to trip her with every step.

But she couldn't slow down; he was gaining on her.

Dammit.

Screw this. She wouldn't be able to keep up this pace through the darkness, and if she knew anything about Chase, it was that he was a relentless S.O.B.

She reached into her jacket for her gun when her head suddenly snapped back, and her feet flew out from underneath her. Pain rocketed through her neck as he yanked her to the ground by her hair.

She hit the ground with a force that knocked the air out of her lungs. Her vision clouded as she tried to blink away the disorientation.

Click.

She knew that sound. Yes, she was very familiar with that sound.

Her senses piqued, her adrenaline spiked. He had her, with a gun pointed directly between her eyes.

Frozen on her back, she inhaled deeply. "Alright, you got me." Despite an effort to sound in control, her voice came out shaky.

"Give me my money, bitch." He stood over her, his face blacked out by the darkness.

Her mind raced.

"Give me my money!"

She narrowed her eyes.

Fuck you.

Adrenaline burst through her veins and she swept her leg along the dirt floor, sweeping him off his feet.

Pop!

A bullet whizzed past her head as she scrambled up, jumped over his body and took off through the woods.

"You bitch!" His scream vibrated through the air, and although she had a head start, she had no doubt he would be close behind her in seconds flat. Sprinting through the woods, she reached back, only to find her gun was gone.

The cold air burned her lungs as she pushed deeper into the woods. Running blind, her foot splashed through a stream of ice-cold water before sliding on a wet rock, knocking her off her feet and into the stream. She pushed herself up, glanced over her shoulder and took off again.

What seemed like forever later, she finally slowed her pace, stopped and strained to listen behind her. Except for the pounding of her heart, the night stood still.

She held her breath and turned. Silence.

Darkness enveloped her as she looked around. Where the hell was she? Out in the middle of freaking nowhere —great.

Suddenly aware she was soaked from the waist down, she shivered and wrapped her arms around herself. She closed her eyes and listened for footsteps, but heard nothing but the hoot of an owl, and the cold breeze through the dead leaves dangling from the trees above.

Maybe he'd given up and turned around.

Maybe not.

Regardless, she needed to find her way back to her car or find some shelter if she was going to survive the night. Which way did she come from? Which direction was the bar?

She realized she had no idea, but knew that she couldn't just stay where she was.

Slowly, she put one foot in front of the other and began walking. The cold air stung her skin through her wet clothes; her joints and muscles stiffening as the temperature began to drop.

After what seemed like an hour, a distant light flickered through the trees. Hope sparked through her and she picked up her pace.

Just beyond a barbed wire fence was a short field and past that, a narrow dirt road with two headlights cutting through the darkness.

Her muscles screamed as she hopped the fence, hunkered down and darted across the field.

As the truck rumbled toward her, she hesitated, but then considering her options, decided to take the risk. It certainly wasn't the first time she'd hitchhiked.

Arm raised—as if she were hailing a damn cab or something—she stepped over the ditch and onto the dirt road. The old, rusted red Chevy slowed, rolled to a stop, and the smudged window rolled down.

"Everything alright, ma'am?" Pushing eighty, at least, the man tipped his Eddie's Farms baseball cap and smiled.

"Yes, sir, I just need a ride. Please."

"I'd be happy to help, ma'am. Hop in."

That was one thing she loved about the South; people were always willing to lend a helping hand, most of the time anyway.

As she jumped in, he asked, "Where to, ma'am?"

"Dave's Bar."

"You got it."

Thirty minutes later she dragged herself up the steps to Barb's B&B and a familiar voice welcomed her from the front porch.

"Well, well, I didn't know you went out this evening. Damn cold, ain't it?"

Barb didn't know the half of it. Jolene shook her head, "Too damn cold to be outside, that's for sure. What are you doing out here?"

"Just laying some food and blankets out for those damn stray cats."

"The same damn stray cats that get into the trash every week?"

Barb nodded.

"Ms. Barb, don't you think if you'd stop feeding them, they'd go find someone else's trash to dig in?"

"My plan is that maybe if I feed them, they'll be too hungry for the trash."

"Might need to rethink that plan."

Barb grinned, giving Jolene the side-eye. "Kind of like how you need to rethink that tattered leather jacket?" She cocked her head. "Honey, are you wet?"

"Yeah, I had a little… incident this evening."

A line of concern ran between Barb's eyebrows. "Incident? You alright?"

She nodded.

"What…" Barb shook her head, "Never mind. I don't even want to know."

Jolene laughed. "No, I don't think you do."

"You must be freezing, bless your heart. Come on in; I'll make you Barb's Special. Extra hot."

"You sure know the way to a gal's heart."

Jolene was welcomed by the smell of sweet vanilla candles, freshly baked bread, and a fire crackling away in the fireplace as she followed Barb inside.

She was home.

Just a stone's throw from Otter Lake, Barb's B&B was a quaint, Victorian-style three story bed-and-breakfast surrounded by lush landscaping, at the end of a narrow dirt road. The house was painted with various shades of cream and beige, and the windows and doors were outlined in bright blue and red. Intricate wood trim and shutters, and a wraparound porch with handcrafted rocking chairs, made the B&B look like a doll house.

A narrow, pebbled path led down to a small cove in the lake, with a dock and two fishing boats for the guests to use at their leisure.

The B&B had become a staple in the small, country town of Berry Springs, Arkansas, nestled deep in the Ozark Mountains.

With a population of just a thousand, Berry Springs was a farmers' town surrounded by soaring, lush mountains, that drew tourists for its picturesque hiking, camping, hunting, and horseback riding. Queens River cut through the south end of town, lending itself to yearlong fishing, canoeing and kayaking, and drained into Otter Lake, just on the outskirts of town.

Nature was as much a part of the town as were the people. And cows.

Berry Springs fit the Southern stereotype to a tee, and its residents wouldn't have it any other way. It was the type of town where hard-work, tradition and family values still meant something. Generations lived on land that their forefathers settled on centuries earlier. Kids grew up playing in the woods and shooting empty Folgers cans with BB guns. The men and women had cowboy hats, and boots, for every occasion.

Loud trucks, tractors, and families on horseback cruised through the town's square, which was home to the post office, Tad's Tool Shop, Donny's Diner, Fanny's Farm and Feed, Anita's Flowers, and Gino's Pizzeria.

Berry Springs was the type of town where people still called each other "sir" and "ma'am" and American flags hung proudly from the light posts.

It was a town where everyone knew everyone, *and* everyone's business.

A country girl at heart, Jolene loved the little town of Berry Springs; and her landlord, Barb, was a big part of that.

Sole owner of Barb's B&B, Barb Stanton was in her mid-fifties—although she'd tell you she was in her forties—and was a fit, quick-witted, tell-it-like-it-is Southern woman who'd relocated to Berry Springs after her husband died twenty years earlier. Always up on the local gossip, Ms. Barb looked like everyone's favorite grandma. She had silver-streaked hair that was always pulled back in a bun, wide-rimmed glasses and hundreds of muu-muu dresses complete with an apron tied over the front. Jolene had been renting Barb's top unit for just over a month and the two had formed a friendly banter.

Jolene followed Barb into the kitchen, grabbed a dish towel and began wiping down her pants and boots.

"Any guests this evening?"

Barb reached into the cupboard and pulled down two

mugs. "Yes, a young couple passing through on their way to a friend's wedding. Mark Williams and Tiffany Lancaster. And we've got some hunters coming in tomorrow."

"Same ones from last week?"

Barb poured steaming hot chocolate into each mug and retrieved the peppermint Schnapps from the liquor cabinet. "Yep. Ol' Bruce caught himself a buck last week; says luck is on his side."

Jolene laughed. "I don't think luck has anything to do with it. I'd say it has more to do with that Ambush Blackout he's shooting with. Hell of a gun."

"Did he show you his guns?"

"No, I saw them loading up last week."

"Ah, I see. Yeah, they bring quite an arsenal. Good guys, though." Barb cocked an eyebrow and glanced over her shoulder. "You ever gonna tell me how it is that you know so much about guns, young lady?"

Jolene smiled. "Maybe someday." Time to change the subject. "Is the young couple staying into the week?"

"No, thank God. Let's just say that I had to put in earplugs last night… and I wore gloves to change the sheets today."

Jolene laughed. "Hey at least someone's getting some lovin' around here."

"Ain't that the truth." Barb sighed and stared blankly out the kitchen window. "Must be nice. Anyway, they book out tomorrow and we'll be vacant the rest of the week." Barb poured two splashes of liquor into the cocoa, and after sliding a glance at Jolene's wet clothes, she splashed a little more. Then whip cream and a sprinkle of cocoa. Barb's Special.

"Mmm," Jolene sipped the warm, smooth cocktail. "Thanks."

"Pretty damn good, ain't it? My granny used to make it for me when I was a little girl."

"Little girl?"

Barb grinned. "Well, close enough to twenty-one, anyway."

"Hey, Barb, Anna."

Greg, the red-headed, freckled-faced cook for the B&B walked in into the kitchen.

"Hey, Greg, what're doing here? You're not scheduled to work today."

"Just swinging by to get my jacket. I left it yesterday."

Barb nodded to the coat rack, next to the door. "I hung it up for you. You'll sure as hell need it with the temperatures dropping this week."

"Thanks. Damn cold outside, no doubt about that." He grabbed his jacket. "Too cold to be pulling bodies from the lake."

Barb's eyes rounded. "What?"

Jolene lowered her drink; her full attention on Greg.

"Y'all didn't hear?" He cocked his head. "You're the queen of gossip, Barb. I figured you'd be the first to know."

"I was busy cleaning your dishes from earlier, son."

He sucked in a breath. "Sorry 'bout that Ms. Barb. Anyway, yeah, just a few hours ago. Chief McCord and his team are still there. Crazy, huh?"

Jolene leaned forward. "They pulled out a *body*?"

"Yep. Well, bones."

Barb put her hand over her chest. "You're kidding? Where?"

"A few miles down."

"Who found it?"

"Old man Ericson; he was out fishing."

"Oh, my God, that's terrible. Do they know who it is?"

"Oh, hell no. According to my buddy in dispatch, it's skeleton bones. All the fish, and God knows what else, ate it bare." He grabbed Barb's drink. "This Barb's Special?"

Barb nodded.

He sipped and continued, "Mmm, so good. Hey, did you hear there's catfish the size of Volkswagens in that lake? Anyway, initial guess is that the body's been down there years. *Years*."

A shiver ran across Jolene's skin as she glanced out the window.

Barb shook her head. "Oh, dear, that's dreadful."

Greg slid into his jacket, and paused for a moment, his eyes darkening. "Makes you wonder what else is at the bottom of that lake. Or... who else."

The room stood still for a moment and a gust of cold air blew the front door open. Wind whipped against Jolene's wet clothes.

Barb shook her head. "Dammit, Greg, you never pull that door closed hard enough."

Jolene picked her drink up from the table. "I'll get it. I'm going to head upstairs to get out of these wet clothes."

Greg frowned. "Wait, what the hell are you doing wet?"

She smirked and narrowed her eyes. "Oh, you know, just hanging out at the lake."

Greg wagged his fingers in the air and in a spooky voice responded, "Ooohhh, so scary, Anna." He laughed.

"I'll admit, you're a bit of a mystery to me, but definitely no murderer."

"Are you sure about that? Sleep with one eye open, little Greggy."

"You know I hate it when you call me that!"

She grinned as she turned and walked out of the kitchen. She closed the front door—tightly—before stepping onto the staircase.

"Hey, Anna?" She stopped, turned, and saw Barb walking down the hall.

"Yeah?"

"Lay out that dreadful leather jacket and I'll see what I can do to clean it off."

"Thanks, Barb."

"Not a problem. Hey, have you decided how much longer you'll be staying with us?"

Jolene sipped her hot chocolate, buying a second of time. "I'm really not sure. I do love it here."

Barb nodded. "Good. No rush at all, honey."

"Thanks."

Jolene turned and started up the staircase, her legs feeling like lead weights with each step. As she passed the second-story landing, she heard the moans and giggling of the young couple, accompanied with the squeaking of bed posts.

As if she needed to hear that to cap off her night.

She took a deep sip of her drink and tried to remember the last time she'd felt the weight of a man on top of her. The warmth of a man's body, the scent of his skin, the wetness of his lips. It had been a long time. A very long time. Too long. But in her line of work, men came and went, usually to jail, or worse. And Jolene was always on the move as well, assuming new identities when the situation called for it. Just like she was now.

When she'd traveled to the inconspicuous town of Berry Springs for a job a month ago, she'd assumed the new identity of Anna Gable—yep, just like Anne of Green Gables. She'd read the book when she was a little girl and it remained one of her favorites today. Reading had always been an escape for her while growing up. Her escape from the chaos, the crime. The fights between her mother and boyfriend. *Boyfriends.*

Over the last few weeks she'd begun to like her new, temporary name.

Things were going smoothly, so far.

She stepped onto the third floor, unlocked her door, and stepped inside. The small, one-bedroom apartment was as quaint and cozy as the rest of the B&B. Cherry oak hardwood floors ran underneath the decorative Native American rugs scattered throughout. A seating area with a couch, end table and television centered the living room. Two large windows overlooking the lake, and a skylight above, allowed the sunshine to light the room. The bedroom and bathroom were just past the kitchen, which was the size of a closet—which didn't bother her much because cooking wasn't her thing. Centered in the bedroom was a luxurious four-post bed with nightstands flanking each side. The bathroom was small with a claw-foot tub, antique sink and a closet in the corner. It was as comfortable as she could ask for, and as much as she hated to leave, she knew she'd have to, soon. Especially after her last job had gone bust and the FBI got involved. She'd lost a lot of money when that damn job fell through.

Jolene was what she would like to call a financial consultant. The government, on the other hand, would accuse her of assisting companies with tax evasion, punishable by up to five years in federal prison.

Her career choice wasn't a surprise, really, considering her upbringing.

Born in a tiny town in Texas, in the heart of the Davey Crockett National Forest, Jolene was the oldest of five children belonging to a young, single, drug-addicted mother with no job, and no interest in raising her children. Jolene had never met her father, and was told he had passed away before she was born. A story that she wasn't sure if she believed.

Jolene found solace from the chaos inside her two-bedoom, one-bathroom home in the woods. Every second that she wasn't in school, she was roaming the mountains.

Jolene grew up as country as they come; playing in the woods, fishing, and hiking. If she wasn't covered in head-to-toe dirt, she didn't consider it a good day.

When Jolene was fifteen years old, her mother met and married a twenty-six-year-old man named Denny Jones. A year later, Jolene woke up one morning to a stack of packed bags in the living room and was told that they were leaving Texas and moving to Denny's hometown of Chicago. In an ironic twist, six months after arriving in Chicago, Denny left her mother after a blowout argument driven by cheating allegations.

To Jolene's dismay, her mother chose to stay in one

of the poorest neighborhoods in Chicago, and not return to Texas.

Jolene could still remember the day her life changed forever. She was sixteen years old and after a night of crying herself to sleep listening to one of her mother's arguments with her most recent boyfriend, Jolene awoke to an abnormally quiet house. She tiptoed downstairs to see her mother, beaten, bloody and passed out on the kitchen floor. Everything in the house was gone, including her mother's boyfriend. After carefully picking up the syringes from the floor so her brothers wouldn't hurt themselves, she stepped over her mother's body and began making breakfast for her siblings. It was that day, that she become the mother, caretaker and provider to four brothers and a thirty-three-year-old woman.

Jolene was a born hustler. Scrappy. Not one to feel bad for herself or wallow in her own misery, Jolene did what was necessary to provide for her family. She began working in a food processing plant at age sixteen where she made a few unsavory acquaintances who taught her that much more money could be made by not following the rules.

By age seventeen, Jolene was the CEO of a little— illegal—side business that she'd created by secretly selling excess product from the plant to local families. During this profitable venture, she learned about tricking the system to make it work for her, and how to manage, multiply, and *hide* financial assets.

At age eighteen, she booked a one-way flight back to Texas and vowed never to return to her life in Chicago again.

Once she arrived in her home state, she did what she knew best. Hustled. She started using her skill set in a small underground cybertheft ring, and it wasn't long before she built a reputation for herself, and was approached by a small manufacturing company to assist in a complex money laundering scheme.

And that's where it all started.

After years of hustling, Jolene had become a highly sought-after financial consultant by some of the country's biggest companies to handle the transferring and hiding of their assets. Her fee was a percentage of the money she handled, and that fee had increased along with her spotless reputation. The hustle paid off, and by age thirty-three, Jolene was financially stable—*very* financially stable—and living life on her own terms.

Exactly the way she wanted it.

Her life was spent traveling from city to city, creating new identities, and stacking her bank account after every job. *Accounts*, that is.

Today, she was Anna Gable residing in Berry Springs, Arkansas.

Tomorrow, who knew?

CHAPTER 2

RELEASING AN EXHALE of exhaustion, Ethan Veech leaned back in his chair and blinked the blurriness from his eyes. The numbers and letters of the code flashing across his computer screen were beginning to merge together.

Caffeine. He needed caffeine.

His eyes darted around the messy cubicle and landed on a coffee mug buried underneath a stack of papers. He cocked his head—he hadn't seen that mug since last year.

He reached forward, knocking three binders on the floor as he grabbed the cup. Empty. Dammit. He wrinkled his nose and peered closer. Was that *fur* growing on the bottom?

Gross.

After tossing the mug in the trash can, he opened his desk drawer hoping to find some loose change, when he heard footsteps behind him.

"Late night and early morning, huh?" Looking as impeccable and authoritative as always, Special Agent Mike Woodson dropped a stack of papers on Ethan's desk.

He shut his desk drawer and rolled back his chair.

"Good morning, sir." He glanced at his watch—6:30. Yes, it was, indeed, another early morning.

Woodson handed him a fresh cup of seven-dollar coffee. "Thought you could use this."

Like a kid on Christmas morning, Ethan's eyes bugged with excitement and he shot his hand forward. "Oh, man, you have no idea."

Woodson smiled and eyed the messy desk. "You know, a file cabinet might help make your late nights run more… smoothly."

"My file cabinet is full with all the assignments you've given me lately. Sir."

Woodson raised his eyebrows and then laughed. "Well, you're proving yourself to be one hell of an up-and-coming computer forensics investigator; I've got to keep you on your toes." He patted him on the back. "All rookies need to start somewhere, Veech. And it's usually under mounds of paperwork. This brings me to why I stopped by. I wanted to tell you what a good job you did on the Stooges case. Tracking them helped save hundreds of lives."

"Thank you, sir."

Woodson nodded. "I also wanted to see if there's been any progress on the Hexagon Group?"

And there it was. The real reason he'd stopped by.

Ethan blew out a breath and shook his head. "Not yet. They've got a hell of a system, or tracker, to cover their tracks. They're playing a game with us. They leave little clues just to throw me off, and then next thing I know I've been tracing something for two damn days that doesn't even exist."

"They can't hack into the Pentagon and expect not to get caught." Pause. "I've got a meeting with the Director at 7:30. This will no doubt come up."

A spike of anxiety shot through Ethan's system. "Give me twenty minutes; I'll put together a spreadsheet of what I've got so far."

"Perfect, thanks." Woodson started to walk away, but turned back around. "Hey, don't you have vacation scheduled this week?"

"Starting tonight, actually." He glanced back at his computer screen. "But I think I'll reschedule, I've got too much on my plate right now."

Woodson shook his head. "No. Take it, Veech. You've earned it. What do you have planned?"

"My girlfriend and I were going to jet off to Aruba, but after she dumped me via text message a few days ago, I canceled the trip."

"Dumped you? Already? Weren't you two only dating a month or so?"

He nodded. "Yep."

"Why'd she hit the road?"

"Something about she never got to see me, and that my only relationship was with work. She ended the text by saying that she hoped that me and the FBI will be very happy together. Whatever the hell that means."

"Damn, I'm sorry, man." Woodson glanced down. "You know, any position with the FBI is going to be a twenty-four-seven job. And… you know that's why my wife left me years ago, too."

Unsure how to handle the brief moment of emotion from the usually stoic agent, Ethan looked down.

"Anyway, I want you to take that vacation. Go to Aruba, Jamaica, or hell, the local bar. Just get out of the damn office for a few days."

"Thanks. I'll think about it, sir."

"Good. Now, before you leave, figure out who the hell is the head of the Hexagon Group and how they hacked into the Pentagon's employee files before you leave."

"Working on it, sir."

Just as Woodson walked away, Ethan's fellow coworker and friend, Agent Jake Thomas stepped up.

"Damn, is everyone working early this morning?"

Ethan took a sip of his coffee and raised the cup. "I always do, Princess."

Jake crossed his arms over his muscular chest. "It's not healthy to be a workaholic, you know."

"Hey, just because I haven't recently found the love of my life and spend every spare second with her doesn't mean I'm a workaholic. Speaking of, how is Dr. Katie Somers?"

Jake smiled. "Good, she's moving here this week."

"Wow, she's leaving NYC for DC—for you—that's quite a move."

"The engagement ring helped speed things along."

"Usually does. Hell, after what you two went through in Berry Springs, I'd bet you guys can make it through anything now."

For a moment, Jakes eyes clouded, and then he nodded.

"Well, I'm happy for you two. Sickened, but happy."

"Thanks, man. Hey, aren't you supposed to be on vacation?"

"Technically at five o'clock tonight."

"Nice. Big plans?"

"Not since Ginger left me."

Jake laughed. "You know, dating a girl named Ginger was your first mistake. Maybe you should date someone who doesn't look like they just slid off the pole next time."

"I always did like shiny things." He laughed.

"Yeah, computers." Jakes eyes suddenly lit up. "Hey, I've got an idea. Why don't you head down to Arkansas for your time off?"

Ethan cocked his head. "To Berry Springs? Why?"

"You could stay in Katie's cabin, for free. She still hasn't sold the place, but it's staged with some nice furniture. Go fishing, hunting, hiking, whatever. The Ozark Mountains are beautiful in the fall. You liked it when you were there, right?"

"Yeah, but I was only there for a few days, helping you on your case." He paused. "Free *is* always good. Did she finish fixing it up?"

"Not all the way."

"I wouldn't mind putting some elbow grease into it to make up for staying there."

"I'm sure she'd appreciate that."

Ethan scratched his chin. "Fishing and a little time in the woods does sound good. And I could meet up with Walker and Jameson for a few beers while I'm in town."

Jake nodded and a minute ticked by.

"Deal."

Jake smiled. "Cool. I'll let Katie know."

Forty-eight hours later, Ethan bounced down the narrow

dirt road of County Road 3228 in his rental truck. Rental *truck*. He was pleasantly surprised that the Northwest Arkansas airport offered trucks.

He gazed out the window at the lush mountains, speckled with orange, yellow and red trees. Even though it was a grey, fall day with thick cloud cover, the darkness seemed to make the bright colors of the leaves stand out even more. Jake was right; the Ozarks were strikingly beautiful in the fall. Being born and raised in west Texas, Ethan didn't get to experience mountains like this.

An only child, Ethan grew up in a blue-collar family where hard work was not only a way of life; it was a necessity to putting food on the table. His mother was his definition of a saint, and his father, his hero. They were an extremely close-knit family and Ethan never took it for granted. His mother was a waitress at the local diner, and his father was a self-employed computer repairman. That's where Ethan got his love for technology. At a very young age, his father took him on calls with him and it wasn't long before he learned the ins and outs of a computer system. But it wasn't until age ten when he saw his first James Bond movie that he knew exactly what he wanted to do when he grew up. He wanted to work in the Cyber Crimes Unit at the FBI.

With the full support of his family, and the tenacity that comes from working for every single thing you get, Ethan created a game plan to achieve his dream and never looked back.

If Ethan wasn't dissecting a computer, he was playing outdoors, hiking, fishing or hunting. He had a love of nature that was second only to his love of computer science.

Ethan graduated valedictorian of his high school and received a full-ride to the state university. He graduated in less than four years, with honors, and a double major in Computer Science and Computer Engineering.

After years of gaining experience by doing internships and hopping around from tech company to tech company, he finally got his chance with his FBI. It was months of interviews, but two years before, Ethan had accepted a computer forensics investigator position within the Cyber Crimes Unit at the FBI.

He loved it, and he was good at it.

Girls, on the other hand, were a completely different story.

A spitting image of his father, Ethan was a muscular six-foot-two, with chestnut brown hair, penetrating hazel eyes and a strong jawline. He never had a problem getting female attention; it was keeping it that was the issue.

Ethan was a born problem solver, a systematic thinker. If anything had a black-and-white answer, he could find it. Even if it took hours, days or months, Ethan could solve a problem. It was anything that wasn't black-and-white, like dealing with emotions, that Ethan had a problem wrapping his head around.

He'd only had one long-term relationship in college, which crashed and burned the moment he took his first job. He put all his time and energy into his work, and wouldn't have it any other way. His job was his life.

Workaholic? Maybe. But he'd finally achieved his dream of working for the FBI and wasn't about to let anything screw it up. Even if that meant being a bachelor for years to come, which didn't settle well with his mother, so he'd promised her that he would settle down one day.

One day.

A light mist coated the windshield as he turned left up the steep driveway that led to the cabin.

Damn, it was chilly, especially for October.

According to the meteorologist, a storm system would bring record-breaking cold temperatures to the Ozarks by the end of the week. Katie and Jake had arranged for the electricity and water to be turned on and plenty of wood delivered prior to his arrival. The old house was built without central air and heat, so he had his work cut out for him keeping a fire lit.

As the truck topped the steep hill, his mouth gaped open at the old rock and log-cabin. Dark shadows from the surrounding woods danced across the yard, which was speckled with dead leaves. Bare tree branches stretched over the roof as if a hand reaching for its prey. The cabin definitely had a "horror movie" feel, but that didn't bother Ethan much; he was never one to be scared of movies. Crooked shutters, a tilted chimney, and a wraparound porch complete with rocking chairs framed the small house.

The one-story cabin looked like it needed more than a little TLC, but it had potential.

Truth was, he was looking forward to time away from work and he would have been happy with a trash can.

He rolled to a stop, turned off the engine, grabbed his bags and stepped out of the truck. A cold gust of wind blew through his jacket as he walked up the crooked steps to the front door. He inserted the key and the door creaked open as he stepped inside.

The dark house was almost as cold as the temperature outside. He sat down his bag and took a look around. The cabin had two front rooms—a den with a stone fireplace and a cozy study—two bedrooms and two bathrooms. The kitchen led out to a back deck with a porch swing. The kitchen was small, but had all the necessities.

He opened the fridge and smiled. A case of beer, enough food to live on, and, *yes*, frozen pizzas in the freezer. He made a mental note to send Jake a thank-you text.

First order of business was to get a damn fire started. No, first order of business was an ice-cold beer, *then* get a fire started. He glanced at the clock on the stove—just after five o'clock. Perfect. He popped the top, took a swig and wandered into the den.

Outside, the dense clouds greedily absorbed what little light was left from the setting sun. He clicked on the television and got to work building a fire.

Thirty minutes and one beer later, Ethan sat back on his heels and admired the raging fire in the fireplace. Not bad. Not bad at all.

He walked to the kitchen, grabbed another beer and headed back to the den.

Now what?

His eyes darted across the room and landed on his brief-case. He'd promised himself that he would only work one, maybe two hours a day during his time off. He'd already spent time on the airplane working, but what the hell, that was in the air, so it didn't count. Right?

He grabbed his laptop and sank into the couch as the fire crackled in front of him. After taking a moment to scan his emails, he opened his file marked *Hexagon Group*. He scrolled through his last notes and took a sip of beer. Why the hell couldn't he penetrate these bastards?

The Hexagon Group had been on the FBI's radar for three years. The group started small with amateur phishing scams and grew quickly. Most recently, they were suspected of hacking a number of government systems, including the Pentagon, and accessing confidential employee files.

Extremely difficult to infiltrate, the group's members were anonymous, loyal, and cloaked in secrecy. Although the intel was shoddy at best, recent information had loosely linked the group to software developer, millionaire Slade Packer and his company, Packer Inc. The problem was, Packer suffered from extreme agoraphobia and never came out from behind the walls of his multi-million dollar mansion in New York City. Very little was known about the man, and it was rumored that only a few people had ever met him. The other problem was that he was rumored to be a literal genius, with expertise in computer science and coding, and his personal and professional life hid behind layers and layers of security. The FBI hadn't had enough reasons to open an official assessment of Packer, but they did take the time to poke around in his affairs—as much as they could without a warrant of course. Packer himself, and Packer, Inc., were clean as a whistle.

But Ethan's gut told him that there was much more to Packer than met the eye.

Ethan was assigned to the Hexagon task force after proving himself on the last case he worked on where he traced a group of anti-government terrorists and saved hundreds of lives. Being assigned to the Hexagon group was no doubt a promotion and he intended on proving himself worthy.

Having already put in close to a hundred man-hours on the case, Ethan had contributed to the arrest of a Belgian man, living in Queens, believed to be tied to the group. Loyal to death, the man exclaimed, he had provided no actionable intel and was being held in a jail cell for an unrelated arrest, where he conned an elderly woman out of her $270,00 savings account. Other than that particular arrest, no advancements had been made to bring down the malicious group or learn more about the mysterious Packer.

The Hexagon Group was beginning to take over Ethan's life. He had to nail the bastards.

More than three hours later, the dwindling fire and chill in the air pulled him away from his computer. He glanced out the window into the darkness. It was a still night, cold, and dark as hell.

As he stoked the fire and prepared for bed, he made his plans for the next day. Maybe a little trout fishing in the morning. Maybe a few beers in the afternoon.

Maybe he'd try to forget about work and enjoy a carefree, uneventful vacation.

Maybe.

CHAPTER 3

HIS HANDS TREMBLED as he poured the wine. His most expensive bottle of red wine. Okay, it was only seventeen dollars, but hell, the local liquor store didn't exactly have a vast selection of wines; what was he supposed to do?

He'd cleaned his apartment from top to bottom the night before, and, just in case, washed his sheets. He'd gone to the liquor store and the grocery store on his lunch break and made a last-minute decision to stop by the flower shop, too. Women loved flowers, right? When faced with the dozens of options in the store, he'd decided to go with tulips. Beautiful, understated, and most importantly, on sale. Sure, his first instinct was red roses, but he thought the romantic flower might give away his true intentions for the evening. It might scare her off. They were only supposed to be friends, after all.

But tonight, he was hoping to change all that.

Greg had obsessed over Debbie as far back as his memories would allow. Kindergarten maybe? Debbie was the most popular girl in school and only dated guys like the star quarterback, not the redheaded smart kid with freckles. Having been adopted when he was younger, Greg had always had self-esteem issues and never felt like he belonged anywhere. Except in Debbie's arms.

It was on one glorious day in chemistry that Debbie sauntered in late to class and was forced to take the only open seat—next to him. He'd almost vomited. But about midway through class, he noticed Debbie copying off of his paper and decided to oblige her by scooting a little closer, so she could see better. Thanks to Greg, Debbie aced the class and they had remained friends ever since.

Only friends.

He grabbed two wine glasses from the cupboard and set them on the table—he'd personally serve her when she arrived—and then took a look around the living room. Candles. Candles would be good.

He lit a few around the room, then checked on the lasagna. Perfect, it was bubbling away and sure to be a hit. Next, the salads. Yep, they were still in the refrigerator right where he left them five minutes ago.

Dammit, why was he so nervous? He felt a sheen of sweat underneath his clothes and ran to the bathroom to apply one more swipe of deodorant, and just a squirt more of his all-over body spray. Zeus, it was called. Boy, he hoped the Gods would be in his favor tonight.

Ding.

His stomach dropped to his feet. The doorbell.

Okay, it's go time.

He glanced in the mirror, gave himself a manly thump on the chest and jogged out of the room.

Slow down idiot, make her wait a second. Don't be so damn eager.

He paused in the entryway for a few beats, and then opened the door.

"Geez, what the hell were you doing, I about froze out there!" Debbie breezed past him and into the apartment. The scent of hairspray and perfume followed seconds later.

"Sorry, I was just in the bathroom."

She wrinkled her nose. "Gross."

Dammit. "Uh, I'll take your jacket."

"Thanks." She slipped out of her coat and handed it to him. He took a second to marvel at the view. Never one to cover up, Debbie sported her signature low-cut shirt, unbuttoned just enough to almost see her bra. *Almost.* Her breasts were perfect. Huge. He didn't understand the big butt craze that was so popular at the moment. He'd take a nice pair of breasts any day. Her bleached-blonde hair was curled and flowing over her shoulders, creating the perfect frame for her red lips and big brown eyes.

"Would you like some wine?"

She popped her gum before saying, "Hell, yeah."

"Have a seat, I'll bring it in."

He took a deep breath as he rounded the corner to the kitchen and grabbed both wine glasses.

"Hey, what's the smell? It smells fantastic."

Yes! "Lasagna. I just threw it together in case you were hungry."

"Wine and lasagna, huh?" She cocked her head as he walked back into the room. "You got a hot date later?"

He laughed a nervous laugh that sounded something

like a cross between a cat choking and a toddler giggling. "Nope, just hanging out with you."

"Well, ain't I lucky?" She popped her gum and winked.

He set the wine glasses on the end table and pulled the movie off the counter.

"Awesome, you got it. I was afraid they'd be sold out."

Little did she know that he'd reserved the latest horror flick she was so anxious to see, *Satan's Island*.

He grinned as he popped it into the DVD player. "Can you handle it?"

"Please. I've been watching scary movies since second grade."

He laughed and threw her the remote. "Get it going, I'll bring some food in."

Moments later they were munching on salads, sipping wine and watching the previews.

He nibbled on a tomato, even though eating was the last thing on his mind. Well, eating food, anyway.

"How was your day?"

She shrugged and sipped her wine. "Not too bad. I got the morning shift at the diner, which was nice."

Donny's Diner was located on the town's square and was a popular spot with the locals; Debbie being the main attraction with the men, of course.

"Do you have to work tomorrow, too?"

Eyes locked on the television, she nodded.

"Maybe I can come by…"

"Shh, it's starting."

Two hours, three dead bodies, and an empty bottle of wine later, the movie credits scrolled across the screen. Greg had strategically turned off the lights after dinner and had spent the entire movie inching as close to Debbie as possible without her noticing.

Now was the time.

She downed the last of her wine and blew out a breath. "That was *freaky*."

His stomach tickled with nerves as he angled himself toward her. He thought about saying *not as freaky as what I'm about to do to you,* but decided against it.

She leaned up from the couch and he quickly slid his hand on her thigh.

"Wait."

She drew her eyebrows together and looked at him. "Wait, what? What's wrong?"

The light from the candle danced in her sultry brown eyes, and his pulse skyrocketed. It was now or never. This was his chance.

Do it.

He ignored the knot in his stomach, licked his lips, leaned forward and kissed her. An explosion of adrenaline burst through his veins the moment their lips touched. She tasted like smooth red wine and marinara sauce. A winning combination in any man's book.

He slid his tongue past her lips, meeting hers in return. A rush of blood between his legs stiffened him like a rock.

"Wait. Wait, Greg." She pulled away.

Breath shallow, he blinked and leaned back, and quickly pulled a pillow over his lap.

"Greg." A confused, yet sympathetic expression washed over her face. "Greg, what are you doing? What are we doing?"

A moment slid by and embarrassment began to replace the excitement between his legs.

"I... um," he paused, wanting the world to open up beneath him and remove him from this humiliating moment. Then, he wasn't sure if it was the embarrassment or the perceived failure of his advance, but he blew out a breath and unloaded years of pent-up emotions.

"Debbie, I've been in love with you since the moment I laid eyes on you. I fell in love with you that day, in chemistry class. When I look at you, I see my dreams, my hopes, my passion standing right in front of me." He leaned forward and touched her hair. "You're the most beautiful woman I've ever seen in my life and I know, without a shadow of a doubt, that no other woman will ever compare to you as long as I'm alive."

Her mouth gaped open.

"Debbie, if you give me a chance, I'll spend every day of the rest of my life making sure you don't regret that decision. I'll keep you happy, love you endlessly and cook you lasagna every night. And if you don't give me a chance, I'll still spend every remaining evening in my life dreaming about you..."

Her eyes bugged, her eyebrows raised. For a moment, she just stared at him, expressionless. But then... she leaned forward and crushed her lips into his, sending her plastic wineglass bouncing on the floor. His heart skipped a beat, his breath caught, before he greedily returned the kiss.

His heart hammered, his head spun. Was this really happening? Yes, it was, and he was going to make the most of every split second.

As their tongues melted together, he reached under

her blouse and wrapped his fingers around her voluptuous breasts. She wore a thin lace bra which did nothing to conceal her erect nipple. His pulse spiked as her hand swept over his leg, flirting with the growing bulge in his jeans.

Touch it. Oh, God, touch it.

And then, she did.

His rock-hard erection pulsated with desire as she rubbed her hand over his jeans. Heat flushed his skin, his whole body radiating with lust.

Unable to take it anymore, he grabbed the ends of her blouse and pulled it over her head. Her breasts spilled over her black, lace bra. He felt paralyzed just looking at her body. The body he had fantasized about for years. *Years.*

He leaned forward, unhooked her bra—saying a thank you to the man above for being able to unhook it so easily—and flung it on the floor. She began fumbling with his belt as he hovered over her, his mouth finding her nipple. He licked, sucked, and nipped as he kicked off his jeans and boxer shorts.

Her hand wrapped around his cock, sending a shot of electricity through his veins.

The dim, blue glow from the television danced across her face as he looked at her. Her beautiful face.

He slid off her lace panties and hovered over her, his cock dangling above her abdomen. For a moment, a rush of insecurity shot through him. The moment he'd dreamed about for so long was about to happen. What if she didn't like it? What if she wasn't impressed? Hell, forget impressed, what if it was awful for her? What if she didn't orgasm?

He shook the thought out of his head and ran his finger down her belly, to her soft pad of hair and onto her inner lips. She was hot with lust, her skin radiating heat. He lightly traced his finger around her before sliding onto her clit. As he softly rubbed back and forth, she leaned her head back and groaned with satisfaction.

Oh, God, he loved that groan.

His erection pulsated and he swore he was the hardest he'd ever been in his whole life. He had to feel her, feel inside her. Deep inside of the woman he'd fantasized about for so long. He held his breath and slid a finger into her. She was so wet. Wet for *him*.

That was it. He couldn't take it anymore.

He trailed his hand back up to her breasts, angled over her, his cock finding her opening.

He looked into her beautiful brown eyes, and with every bit of passion he had in him, he slid into her. Her warmth enclosed tightly around him and he was overtaken with the sensation.

He closed his eyes and bit his lip as he slowly slid in, out, in and out.

He was already about to explode.

"Wait."

His eyes shot open.

Breathless, she said, "Wait."

He stopped. His heart stopped.

She scooted out from under him, her face flushed with emotion. "Greg, what are we doing?"

His stomach sank. His world stopped.

She grabbed her shirt and panties, and sat up. Under her breath, she muttered, "Oh, my God."

He grabbed a pillow and covered himself.

She slid on her shirt and took a deep breath. "Greg,

what the hell are we doing?" She looked at him, her eyes almost frantic. "Look… I like you, Greg, I do. But… just as friends."

He. Wanted. To. Die.

She started to say something else when her phone rang. Her hands were unsteady as she reached for it.

"Hello… hey girl… yeah, um," she glanced at Greg, then back at the floor, "hold on."

She pulled the phone down and looked at him; her big brown eyes sympathetic. "I've got to go pick up Tracey from the bar. She and Curt got into a fight, again. Um," she paused, "I'm sorry about what happened, I mean, for kissing you back and for everything. I shouldn't have. I… let's just keep this thing as friends, alright?"

His mouth gaped open. He was in total shock; completely engulfed in embarrassment and inadequacy. Was it him? Was it the kiss? *Oh, God*, was it the size of his package? His stomach churned as he looked back at her. Unable to even form a sentence, he just nodded.

"Good." She slid into her clothes and all but bolted off the couch. Grabbing her purse, she said, "Good night, Greg."

As she stepped out of his front door, he heard her laugh and say into the phone, "Oh, my God, girl, you'll never believe what just happened…"

CHAPTER 4

ETHAN KICKED HIS boots on the side of the house, dislodging the caked mud before walking into the cabin.

A cool gust of wind swept up his back, sending a chill up his spine. The cold front was already starting to creep in and he hadn't anticipated how cold it was really going to be. This was the *South* wasn't it? Sheesh.

He'd woken up to his alarm clock screaming at him at five o'clock in the morning.

Setting the alarm the night before had seemed to be good idea at the time—after a six-pack. But even though he was tired, the trip proved to be bountiful as he set the cooler filled with five trout on the kitchen counter.

His stomach growled reminding him that it was lunchtime, but first order of business was to brew a hot cup of coffee to thaw out his insides.

He peeled off his gloves before sitting down and removing his heavy hiking boots. His feet were stiff from the cold and ached from hiking the terrain, but he loved being out in the woods, in nature, and he was glad he'd gone.

Being an outdoorsman to the soul, he felt right at home in the beautiful Ozark Mountains. On his hike to the river, he'd seen six deer, two foxes and even a bald eagle. The thick woods lining the mountains were part of a thriving ecosystem filled with caves, streams, rivers, bluffs and cliffs as high as three-thousand feet. Black bears, mountain lions, coyotes and elk were just a few inhabitants of the woods. In Berry Springs, Arkansas, the mountains were a way of life, and were to be respected and preserved.

He was surprised how many people he passed and even a few brave kayakers were on the river. He'd stopped and chatted with a few locals out on their first deer hunt of the season, who offered him a sip of their peppermint schnapps before parting ways. It was only polite to accept.

And now, it was only midday and he was officially beat.

He pushed off the chair, set the coffee to brew and had to stop himself from powering up his laptop to get in a few hours of work. *You're on vacation*, he thought.

As the coffee pot spit and hissed, he wasn't quite sure what do with himself.

This was ridiculous. What do most men do on vacation? Relax and have a few beers. That's right. That's exactly what he'd do.

He poured himself a cup and grabbed his cell phone.

"Jameson here."

"Hey, Jameson, it's Ethan Veech."

"Well, I'll be damned, how the hell are ya?"

"Doing good, just taking a little time off of work."

"Yeah? Where to?"

"Good ol' Berry Springs, Arkansas."

"No shit? You're here?"

"Yep, Jake and Katie offered their cabin for free, so here I am."

"Can't beat that. We need to meet up for a beer while you're in town."

"My thoughts exactly. Just tell me when and where."

"How about eight o'clock tonight, Frank's."

"See ya then."

Click.

He tossed his phone on the counter and glanced around the cabin. He'd promised Jake that he would earn his keep by working on a few things around the place while he was there. And if there was anything he knew better than computer analytics, it was handyman work. Growing up, his father always said: *why pay someone to do something when you can do it yourself?* And he was right.

His gaze landed on his laptop and after a moment's hesitation, he decided to check his email before beginning an afternoon filled with manual labor.

He topped off his coffee, sat at the kitchen table and powered up his computer. After a million log-ins and security scans, he filtered through emails and then opened his Hexagon file.

Slade Packer.

He needed to learn more about the mystery man, so that he could either investigate further or cross him off his list of possible suspects responsible for hacking into the Pentagon.

He needed more.

A week ago, he had tracked an IP address that was presumed to belong to Packer, but the moment he started poking around in it, it went offline and hadn't been active since. There was also that pesky little thing called privacy laws to worry about, but Ethan didn't give that too much thought—never had when it came to solving a mystery.

He opened one of his trusted programs and typed in the IP address, for the hundredth time.

Online.

Online?!

He almost fell out of his chair.

His pulse picked up as his fingers flew over the keyboard looking for open ports to access the computer.

Denied, denied, denied.

Shit.

He sat back, sipped his coffee and decided to go a different route, and test out a program he had built himself— an alternative, more advanced program to search for any points of entry.

He ran the IP address again, nothing.

Dammit.

His wheels turned as he stared at his screen, sipping his coffee.

He spent the next hour tweaking his program, and decided to run the IP address one last time before giving up.

Bingo.

His heart stopped. He was in. Holy SHIT!

He wagged his fingers, releasing the adrenaline pumping through his veins before diving in. He blinked and leaned forward. Everything was encrypted. Every single damn thing.

"Okay, I can work with this," he muttered as he started scanning the programs and documents.

And then, the screen went black and a skull with cross bones popped up.

"*Shit.*"

He slammed the screen shut and blew out a breath.

∽

Beep, beep. Beep, beep.

Beep, beep. Beep, beep.

The black leather chair turned and the alert *SYSTEM BREECH* lit up the screen. Slade Packer cocked an eyebrow and peered at the screen. The FBI.

Having been pre-programmed to automatically trace any breach, the computer began racing with code, programs and scans until the intruder's name flashed on the screen.

Ethan Veech, FBI, Cyber Crimes Unit. IP location, Berry Springs, AR.

∽

Seven hours later, Ethan walked into Frank's Bar and Grill.

Greeted by a jangling cowbell that hung above the door, the restaurant was quintessential Southern dining at its finest. He absolutely loved it.

Dark hardwood covered the floors, mismatched tables scattered the room, and red booths lined the walls. Rusted road signs and deer antlers decorated the wall behind the bar, which was surrounded by bright red barstools. In the back were a few pool tables, and a dance floor sat in front of a small stage. A continuous stream of good ol' country music floated from the jukebox. Damn, he loved country music. *Old* country music, not the crossover pop country that was so big nowadays. These new artists—as they called themselves—couldn't hold a candle to Willie Nelson or Merle Haggard, in his eyes.

Frank's Bar was within walking distance of the police station, which made it a regular cop hangout.

He spotted Jameson at the bar, in his signature worn, brown leather jacket.

"Hey, Veech, good to see you, man." Jameson stood and they shook hands.

"You, too, Jameson." He slapped him on the back before sliding into the stool next to him.

While Ethan was in town weeks earlier, he and Detective Jameson struck up a friendship and capped off every evening meeting with drinks at Frank's, discussing the case they were working on, and, unrelated, the enigma of women. Jameson was a dark-haired, dark-eyed Army veteran, and had been on the Berry Springs police force for twelve years before getting promoted to detective.

"Howdy, whatcha drinkin'?"

Linda, a young, bleached-blonde bartender with hair teased six-inches high walked up and wiped her hands on her apron. The saying *the bigger the hair, the closer to God,* ran through his head.

"Beer. Shiner, please. And a cheeseburger and fries."

"How would you like that cooked?"

"Rare."

"You got it."

He glanced at the detective's half-empty highball drink. "Rough night?"

Jameson shook his head and took a sip.

The waitress delivered Ethan's beer. "Thanks." He turned back to his friend. "What happened?"

"Nothing earth-shattering… just got the brush off from a girl I had just started seeing."

He took a deep gulp of his beer. "Why?"

"Oh, something about she's sick of having a relationship with my cell phone."

He exhaled. "Sounds familiar. Didn't you tell her being involved with a cop is tough?"

"Yep, on our first date. She was fine with it then, but not anymore, apparently." Jameson shook his head. "I take it home with me, man. The work. The drama. The bodies."

Ethan looked down, knowing that the comment didn't need a response.

After a moment, Jameson gulped the last of his drink and motioned to the waitress for another round. "Here's to failed relationships. Or, hell, ones that never even made it off the ground."

The waitress delivered Ethan's cheeseburger and Jameson's drink.

"Did you hear about the human remains we found in Otter Lake last night?"

Ethan raised his eyebrows. "No, missed that news."

"Yep, found three arm and leg bones, and a clavicle bone. Washed up on shore."

"You're sure it's human?"

"Yep, our local Medical Examiner—Jessica, I think you met her while you were here—confirmed it. She estimated that the bones have been in the water for years."

"Years, huh?"

"Yep."

"Skull?"

"Nope. Divers went down today and haven't found anything else so far. We'll keep at it."

"Damn. Anything you can tell from the bones so far?"

Jameson shook his head. "Not initially. There's marks all over them, but there's no doubt that most, if not all, are from fish and whatever else gnawed on them."

"Could be knife marks."

"That's a possibility. The forensic anthropologist will determine that. We're sending the bones off to the state crime lab for further analysis."

That was the drawback of being a small-town cop—lack of resources. The Berry Springs police department was small-town, Southern law enforcement at its best. The department had a grand total of three officers, not including the Chief of Police, and one detective.

"Anyone missing that rings a bell?"

"Nope."

"Well, shit."

"Exactly."

They sat in silence for a moment, both imagining what could have happened to the owner of the bones, as their brains were trained to do.

Eventually, Jameson sipped his drink and looked at Ethan. "So how's the FBI?"

"Good, but I'm damn ready to drop the 'rookie' label."

"Gotta crawl before you walk."

He nodded and sipped his beer. "They've assigned me to a pretty high profile case… you heard of the Hexagon Group?"

"The Hexagon Group? Yeah, I think so. Aren't they the

ones who hacked into the employee files of the Pentagon a few months ago?"

"Exactly. They're an extremely talented group. I've spent God knows how many hours tracking them and have gotten nowhere substantial."

"Any leads at all?"

"Slade Packer ring a bell?"

He cocked his head, searching his memory. "Nope."

"He's a millionaire software developer. A recluse. Been linked to the group as potentially the leader."

"A millionaire recluse. Sounds ominous."

Their attention was drawn to loud voices around the pool tables in the back. Just cowboys betting on a pool game.

Ethan shook his head. "Anyway, I'm trying like hell to keep from working on it during my vacation."

Jameson laughed. "If there's anything I learned about you the last time you were in town it's that you're a hell of a computer whiz, and one hell of a workaholic."

He raised his glass. "The Veech legacy continues."

"Hey, Jameson... son of a bitch, Ethan Veech, what the hell are you doing here?"

In full uniform, Officer Dean Walker slid into the stool next to Veech.

"Hey, Dean." They shook hands. "Just in town on a little vacation."

"Nice. I was hoping you weren't here on another damn case again."

"Not this time."

"Well, it's damn good to see you. How you been?"

"Can't complain."

Like a schoolgirl, the waitress practically fell over herself when she spotted Dean. "Hey, Dean, how are you, I mean what can I get for you?" Ethan swore her cheeks flushed as she addressed the officer.

Dean smiled, "Hey, Linda. How are you this evening?"

Fumbling with her apron, she batted her long, painted eyelashes and said, "Oh, I'm good. Same ol' same ol'."

"Did you do something different with your hair?"

"I curled it."

"Looks nice."

She giggled and smoothed her hair. "Thank you. So, um, what'll you be having?"

"I'll take a Shiner, please."

She smiled, "Comin' right up."

Jameson chuckled and leaned forward, "Hey, Walker, can you hand me that napkin? I need to wipe her drool up off the bar."

Dean glanced down at the bar, "Hmm, I don't know Jameson, it actually looks like happy tears from your old lady after she kicked you to the curb."

Ethan snickered.

"Damn, man, how'd you hear about that already?"

"It's Berry Springs; everyone knows everything about everyone. How you holdin' up?"

"Whiskey helps."

"Always does, brother."

Born and raised in Berry Springs, Dean Walker's six-foot-four muscular body was enough to intimidate every man that crossed his path. It was also enough to make almost every woman drop to her knees. Well, that, and his movie star good looks. Dean had dark hair and emerald green eyes that made him popular with the girls his whole life. He grew up a farm boy, a real Southern cowboy, working on the family farm from dawn until dusk, every minute that he wasn't in school.

He'd joined the police force six years ago and now, his weekends were filled running the farm, and his weekdays, working the beat. He wouldn't have it any other way.

The front door opened and the sound of high heels rang like a catcall through the air.

Jameson smirked. "Oh, man."

"Oh, man, what?" Ethan looked over his shoulder. "Diner Debbie."

Every hot-blooded male was gawking at the blonde as she sauntered through the bar. It took Ethan a minute for his eyes to make it up to her face, but once they did, her eyes locked on his. He looked back at Jameson.

"Who's Diner Debbie?"

"Just Debbie. She works at the diner, so it's a convenient, and rather insulting, if you ask me, nickname. Here she comes."

"Howdy, boys."

Debbie and her friend, Tracey, flanked either side of the three men.

"Hey, Debbie, Tracey. How are y'all?"

"Good." She looked at Ethan. "I don't believe we've met."

Jameson cleared his throat. "Oh, sorry, this is Ethan Veech."

She smiled, a twinkle in her eye. "Hey, Ethan, I'm Debbie."

"Nice to meet you."

"What brings you to little ol' Berry Springs?"

"Vacation."

"Nice. And how do you know these two rednecks?"

"We've worked together in the past."

She raised her eyebrows. "You a cop?"

He shook his head.

Jameson took a swig of his drink. "Oh, now, don't be modest. Ethan here works for the FBI."

Her eyes rounded. "Seriously? The FBI?"

"Just in cybersecurity, I'm no hero like these two badasses." He slapped Jameson on the back and winked.

"Wow, that's so cool."

Jameson and Walker both rolled their eyes. Something about a secret agent, or close to at least, made women go nuts.

Ethan sat up a little straighter in his chair and tried to avoid the smirks from his buddies.

"Tracey and I are gonna grab a drink. Maybe you guys can play us in a game of pool later?" She winked. "If you don't mind getting your asses beat."

Dean set his beer on the bar shook his head. "Uh-uh, Miss Debbie. You're already fifty dollars in the hole with us already."

She wrinkled her nose. "Dammit, I was hoping y'all would let that slide."

"No, ma'am, a bet's a bet."

She laughed and tossed her hair over her pointy shoulder. "Double or nothing?"

"You're on."

CHAPTER 5

TWO HOURS AND three beers later, Dean and Jameson were collecting four twenty dollar bills from Tracey when Debbie walked over to Ethan.

She grabbed his beer, sipped, then said, "You're pretty good with a stick."

"You're pretty good with the innuendos."

She laughed and raised her drink. "Damn whiskey. Sorry."

He laughed.

"So how long you here for?"

"Just a few days."

She leaned against her pool stick. "As a Berry Springs local, it's my duty to make sure your stay here is everything you'd want it to be."

He raised his eyebrows. Wow, this girl was something else. "Oh, yeah? And how do you plan to do that?"

"By taking you out for some good ol' Southern barbecue, and a few beers."

"You know I'm from Texas, right?"

She shook her head, "Oh, don't start that with me. Arkansas barbecue can run circles around Texas."

Buying some time to consider his answer, he sipped his beer, eyeing her over the rim. She certainly wasn't bad to look at. And hell, he *was* on vacation. Isn't that what vacation is all about? Having fun and saying "yes" to adventures? And beautiful women?

Yes.

He tipped up his drink. "You're on."

She winked. "You won't regret it."

Just then, the front door opened. A gust of wind swept up her back, sending her dark hair whipping around her face as she walked into the bar.

Her worn leather jacket draped over a tall, slender frame with feminine hips and a killer ass. But something told him that feminine was not a word this woman would use to describe herself. She was absolutely stunning, alluring.

She didn't look around, searching for any particular man or woman, instead, she walked with confidence, straight to the bar. He had no doubt that she was the kind of woman who was content to be alone. He watched her slide onto a barstool and remove her jacket, and something stirred in him. What, he wasn't sure, but he definitely had a reaction to this woman. Had he met her before?

He looked closer. Her long, dark hair looked like silk against her flawless skin. Her lips were a rosy pink and had that sexy, pouty thing going on, and she had deep brown eyes that he guessed didn't miss much.

And written all over that incredible face was the message—*fuck you.*

Yep, she was one of the most beautiful women he'd ever seen.

She draped her jacket on the stool next to her, flagged down the waitress and ordered a drink. He made a quick bet with himself that she'd ordered liquor, not beer.

"Helllooo?"

Ethan snapped back to reality. How long had he been staring?

Debbie cocked her head. "You alright?"

"Yeah. Yeah, sorry."

"Good. Wanna play another game before calling it a night?"

He glanced back at the woman at the bar, pulling at him like a magnet.

"No thanks. I think I'm going to grab another drink. Be right back."

Without waiting for a response, Ethan grabbed his beer and drained it as he maneuvered through the tables. An old Willie Nelson song danced through the air as he slid in between two barstools, one down from her. Not too close, and not too far away.

Her gaze remained focused on the old television behind the bar that was showing an African safari documentary about a male cheetah stalking an oblivious, female gazelle.

He pretended to look at the front door and slid her another glance. Damn, she *was* familiar. Where the hell had he seen her before?

The waitress walked up. "Another beer?"

"Please."

"You got it."

As the waitress scurried off, he looked over, this time

directly at her. Her eyes remained on the television as she sipped her Jack and Coke.

"Five bucks he gets her."

Without glancing over, she said, "Make it a hundred."

He raised his eyebrows and accepted the challenge. "You're on."

They watched the fierce cat slither through the brush, its eyes locked on his prey. His slow, confident movements went unnoticed by the herd. As the cat inched closer, the gazelle's head snapped up. The cat crouched, then shot out of the brush like a cannon through the air. The gazelle took off, and the herd scattered. The background blurred as the two animals ran across the plain. Closer, closer, the cat was less than two feet behind her. She raced, full-force, occasionally pivoting to throw off her prey. And then, finally, the cheetah slowed his pace and backed off.

The gazelle won.

Wide-eyed, Ethan glanced over at his adversary. The corner of her lip curled into a smirk.

"Dammit."

Her eyes remained on the television. "That'll be a hundred bucks. Please."

He reached into his wallet, slapped a hundred dollar bill on the bar, and slid onto the stool next to her.

"I'da made that bet ten times out of ten. Cheetahs are the fastest animals on earth."

"Apparently not."

He smiled, assessing her. "Yes, apparently not."

She sipped her drink.

"Are you into abnormally fast African creatures?"

"Not necessarily, but," she gave him the side-eye, "never bet against a woman."

"Lesson learned."

"Glad I could help."

He smiled and sipped his beer. The woman was definitely a formidable opponent.

"Do I know you from somewhere?"

For the first time, she turned and fully looked at him, her dark eyes narrowed. "I don't think so."

"Are you sure? I swear I recognize you."

"Maybe I just have one of those faces."

No, she definitely didn't have just one of those faces. Her face should be on a runway in New York City.

He reached out his hand. "I'm Ethan."

She slid her soft hand over his and gripped. His stomach tickled.

"Anna."

"Nice to meet you, Miss?"

"Gable."

"Gable? Anna Gable? You're joking."

"Is that funny, Mr...?"

"Veech. Ethan Veech. And kind of. Ever read Anne of Green Gables?"

"About a million times. And yes, the coincidence is not lost on me, or nearly every person I meet."

"Alright, well, I'm glad we cleared that up."

They both stared ahead, unsure how to tackle the first small-talk hurdle they had just reached.

Ethan cleared his throat. "Do you live here?"

She paused. "Temporarily."

"Where are you from?"

"Around."

Okey doke. He could take a hint. He grabbed his beer and started to stand when Debbie's six-inch heels stopped behind them.

She draped her arm around Ethan and glanced at Jolene. "I don't believe we've met."

Jolene cocked an eyebrow and slowly glanced over, and an awkward silence weighed the moment. Ethan looked back and forth between the two. At first glance the two women were polar opposites of each other, almost comically so. Like Batman and Robin. If Robin had enormous boobs, bleached-blonde hair and the ability to drink most men under the table.

"Well," Debbie smacked her gum. "I'm Debbie."

"Anna."

"Nice to meet you. How do you know Ethan?"

"I don't."

Annoyed at the mystery woman's aloofness, Debbie smacked her gum a few more times, turned to Ethan and under her breath said, "You have fun with all that." She rolled her eyes and sauntered away.

Jolene gulped the last of her drink, stood and grabbed her jacket. "Nice to meet you, Ethan Veech." She stuffed the hundred dollar bill in her pocket and winked. "Very nice."

He smiled as she turned and walked out the front door, and under his breath said, "Miss Anna Gable, it was a pleasure to meet you as well."

Another hour later, Ethan glanced at his empty beer bottle, at the clock, and then at Debbie who was mid-way through her third game of darts with Dean and Jameson. He glanced at the door, hoping that Anna Gable had decided to come back and watch more on the animal network.

Nope.

He set down his beer bottle and stood. Time to head home.

"Well, guys, I'm outta here."

Debbie looked over while releasing a dart in the air, narrowly missing Dean's face.

"Now? Why so soon?"

"Fish bite best at dawn."

She walked over. "You consider waking up at the ass crack of dawn and going out in the freezing weather to fish, a vacation?"

He smirked and nodded.

She shook her head. "Boy are we going to have fun when we go out." She laughed. "Come on, I'll walk you out."

After waving at Dean and Jameson, who winked and made a few obscene gestures while Debbie wasn't looking, he followed Debbie out of the front door.

The crisp air swept through his jacket as he stepped outside. The glow of the moon illuminated the gravel parking lot. It was a clear, cool night.

"Where'd you park?"

"Back corner, over here."

Debbie wrapped her arms around herself as they walked across the parking lot.

"Dammit, it's *freezing* outside."

Ethan shrugged. "I'll take cold over a hundred degrees any day." He motioned to the truck. "Here I am." He unlocked the door and turned toward Debbie.

She smiled. "It was a pleasure meeting you tonight."

"You, too."

"I'll call you tomorrow; we'll plan our barbecue date."

"Looking forward to it."

And then, without warning, she leaned up on her tiptoes and kissed his cheek. "Night."

"Night."

He watched her saunter away before sliding behind the steering wheel and starting the engine.

As he rumbled out of the gravel parking lot, he didn't notice the figure step out from behind the shadows, and watch his truck fade into the distance.

CHAPTER 6

ETHAN WAS SLAPPED in the face by frigid air as he stepped into the cabin. Dammit, he'd forgotten to stoke the fire before he met the boys for a drink. He grabbed a pair of gloves from the windowsill and started back outside.

The woodpile sat across the yard against the tree line and he shivered as he stepped through the dark night.

A black cat darted out from behind a log and scurried into the woods, scaring him half to death.

He grabbed an armful of logs and headed back to the house.

As he walked up the steps, he heard the rumble of a truck inching down the dirt road. He paused and turned. In the short time that he'd been here, he hadn't heard a single vehicle drive past the cabin. He wasn't sure where the dirt road ended but he figured it wasn't too far past the house. He looked down the hill at the dim lights cutting through the darkness.

Slowly, the truck turned into the driveway and stopped. What the hell?

He turned fully around now, assuming that whoever was in the truck could see the outline of his body against the light from the cabin. Something sent a warning bell through his system as he stared at the truck, and its driver back at him.

He squinted, trying to make out the model. As far as he could tell it was an older, red, single cab truck.

Finally, the reverse lights came on and the truck backed slowly out of the driveway and drove off in the same direction it had come from.

He stood on the porch until he heard the engine fade into the darkness.

Humph. Maybe some kids looking for a secluded spot to do God knows what. Who knows?

He turned, walked into the house and straight to the den to stoke the fireplace.

Ten minutes later a fire raged in front of him as he sank into the couch and flicked on the television.

Sports, news, late-night talk shows, cooking shows.

He was bored.

His gaze landed on the laptop sitting on the coffee table. After a moment's hesitation, he leaned forward and grabbed it.

He rolled his eyes and shook his head. He sure as hell wasn't doing a great job of not working on his vacation.

He logged into his computer and after several security verifications later, he was in his email.

He skimmed through the top few and opened the first one from Mike Woodson with the subject "Hexagon Group."

The email was an update on Mike's meeting with the

director, and he was right, the subject of the notorious hacking group did come up. Apparently, Slade Packer had realized that someone from the FBI had hacked into his system, and his lawyers fired off a letter demanding that a federal warrant must be obtained before they probe into his life any more than they already had. Apparently, Packer had as many lawyers as he did dollars.

Ethan sat back and ran his fingers through his hair. How the hell can he get to this guy?

After an hour of replying to emails and skimming reports, he closed his laptop and glanced at the clock. Almost midnight. He was beat.

He pushed off the couch, added more wood to the fire and made his way into the bedroom. He glanced out the window into the darkness. It was going to be a cold night. Damn cold. He considered grabbing a blanket and sleeping next to the fire, but decided to tough it out. A king-size bed is a hell of a lot more comfortable than hardwood floors.

He stripped out of his clothes, stepped into a pair of flannel pajama bottoms, flicked off the light, and slid into bed.

All in all, he'd had a good day. Fishing in the morning, beers with the boys in the evening, and he'd even been asked out on a date by the hottest girl in town.

Well, second hottest.

He closed his eyes.

She said her name was Anna. Anna Gable. He chuckled. What a name. He definitely would have remembered that name, so why the hell did she look so familiar to him? Had they met somewhere before?

Her image popped into his head. Her long, dark hair,

flawless skin, and big, alluring brown eyes. But it wasn't just the sex appeal; it was the juxtaposition of her beautiful appearance and her badass, don't-mess-with-me persona. He'd always had a thing for strong women and he had no doubt that this woman knew how to handle a situation.

He rolled on his side and took a deep breath.

It was bugging the hell out of him that he couldn't place her.

He took another deep breath and, with her image locked in his head, drifted to sleep.

Hours into his deep sleep, he began to dream. He dreamt of Anna Gable, in a string bikini frolicking on a beach. He dreamt in black and white—like a grainy surveillance photo.

Like a photo taken by a secret agent.

His eyes shot open.

Jolene Reeves.

Anna Gable was Jolene Reeves, who was under surveillance by the FBI.

Holy *shit*. Anna was Jolene. Jolene was Anna. There was no doubt about it. His pulse picked up and he sat up. He couldn't believe it.

He glanced at the clock—six-thirty in the morning. He knew he should inform Woodson that he'd found her. But for some reason, that thought made his stomach sink. Why?

He shook the thought away and reached for his phone.

Would they send someone down to arrest her on the spot? Or, would the local PD toss her in jail for a few days first?

He clicked his phone on, scrolled down the call list and clicked on Special Agent Mike Woodson.

He hesitated.

Why the hell did he hesitate? He glanced out the window where the dim light of dawn was beginning to cut through the trees. Maybe he should wait until he was one-hundred percent sure that it was her before he goes ringing the bell at the FBI. That made sense, right?

Right.

He set down the phone, flung the covers off and pushed out of bed. The house was dark and cold. He slid into a pair of Levi's, skipped the shirt and walked into the kitchen to set the coffee to brew. As the pot began to gurgle, he stoked the fire and grabbed his laptop when his phone rang.

"Veech here."

"Veech, it's Miller."

Matt Miller, a fellow computer forensics geek, was in his tenth year working for the FBI and had been assigned as Ethan's mentor. Matt was a divorced, thirty-seven-year-old father of one. It was marriage or the job, the wife had said, and he chose the job.

For a fleeting moment, Ethan considered telling Matt about his run-in with the beautiful criminal, Jolene Reeves. But that thought lasted less than a second.

"Hey, Matt what's up?"

"Oh, you know, just livin' it up behind the grey walls here at the HQ."

"They really do need to paint those damn walls."

"I'll let Mike know."

"It's early. Did you call to talk about walls?"

"In a manner of speaking, yeah. You penetrate the wall of security around the Hexagon Group yet?"

Ethan released an exhale. "No, man, not yet."

"I wanted to let you know that it's starting to grow legs. It's on the director's radar now."

"Yeah, I heard."

"That dude, Packer, is like a mythical creature. A dragon, hidden away in a lair of hundred dollar bills. Never to be seen or heard from; but you know he's there."

"Kind of like Smaug."

Matt laughed. "Nice Lord of the Rings reference. But what a horrible cliché."

"What? Computer geeks sitting on the phone talking code and quoting LOTR?"

"Exactly."

Ethan grinned and switched back to the subject. "Do we have any other information on him other than what's in the file?"

"Nope. And that's the other reason I called. Because this is getting such visibility, I want you to solely focus on Packer. Find out everything about him, without getting caught of course. I'll work on it on my end, too."

Ethan glanced out the window. "I already got busted hacking into his computer."

"Shit, you know how many times I've got busted for that?"

Ethan laughed. "You know I'm always up for a challenge."

"After your vacation, of course."

He glanced at his open laptop. "Of course."

"Speaking of, how's Arkansas? Did you get your overalls and straw hat yet?"

"Yep. Borrowed them from your mom."

"Very funny."

"No, seriously, it's great down here this time of year. Beautiful." He thought of Jolene.

"You meet up with the Berry Springs PD yet?"

"Yeah, had beers last night."

"How are they doing?"

"Good. Pulled a few bones out of the lake last night, so that's big news."

"Human bones?"

"Yeah."

"Hmm, interesting. Anything else interesting?"

It was almost like Matt was asking Ethan to tell him about Jolene. He began pacing the room. "Nope. That's about it."

"Alright, man. Have fun down there, let me know if you need anything."

"Will do, buddy. Thanks."

Ethan set his phone on the counter, grabbed his laptop and powered it up. He logged into the FBI file database and scrolled down to the file named *Jolene Reeves*. He double-clicked and his screen filled with various documents, telephone screenings, and surveillance photos. He clicked on the first photo and her face filled the screen.

Her beautiful, sultry face.

Yep, Anna was definitely Jolene.

He minimized the photo, clicked through a few of the documents and confirmed what he already knew. Jolene was suspected of being involved in a small cybertheft ring, years ago. And was suspected of being a tax evasion specialist for hire, and part of a bigger, underground network of like-minded criminals. The FBI was more interested in finding out who she worked for, instead of arresting her—

which would have been impossible anyway because they couldn't prove any wrongdoing thus far. Jolene was a pro at covering her tracks. She was smart.

However, that all had changed a few weeks earlier when Jolene pulled a gun on a fellow FBI agent during a standoff at the Arkansas State Capitol Building. She got away and now they wanted to bring her in.

He sat back and laughed. They must not have been looking very hard for her, if a simple name change had thrown them off. Bigger fish to fry, he guessed.

The coffee pot dinged and he pushed out of the chair, grabbed a mug, and filled it to the top. He sipped; the hot liquid warming his insides. He walked back to his laptop and began closing it down, but stopped on the file titled Slade Packer.

His hand froze, his wheels began to turn.

Slade Packer. Millionaire software developer suspected of running an underground hacking group.

Jolene Reeves. Sultry, sexy vixen also suspected of being involved in an underground network of white -collar criminals.

Hacking… cybertheft… money laundering… did they cross paths?

Does she possibly know Slade Packer?

Shit, is it possible that she works for him?

No way.

Deep in thought, Ethan glanced outside. The early morning sun peeked over the tallest mountain, making for a picturesque morning. He grabbed his coffee and stepped outside, onto the porch. The cool, crisp air swept across his shirtless chest and carried with it the unmistakable scent of fall. The woods surrounding the cabin danced in the breeze, colorful leaves floating to the ground. Gold beams of sunlight burst over the mountaintop and just beyond the field were four deer, blending perfectly into their surroundings. The sky above was a cloudless blue, promising for a clear day ahead.

Goosebumps broke over his skin as he sipped the hot coffee, and in the distance he could hear the babble of a nearby stream.

He inhaled. Work could wait.

Fishing. It was a good day for fishing.

Jolene's phone jangled in the seat next to her and she rolled up the car window to block out the noise.

She'd spent the day at a nearby town, known for its eclectic art shops. She'd always appreciated art and had collected many pieces from all the countries she'd visited. All of which were sitting in a storage unit in Texas. Before she knew it, the day had faded into evening and it was already eight o'clock.

"Hello?"

"Jolene, hey, it's Dylan."

"Dylan, to what do I owe the pleasure?"

"A new job offer."

Jolene clicked on her turn signal and pulled into the B&B driveway.

She turned off the car. "Okay, what's the offer?"

"Have you heard of Beckett Industries?"

"Sure, they're a private contractor for the military, right? Manufacture weaponry. Based in New York, right?"

"Right. Well, they've secretly contracted with someone overseas and need to hide a portion of the profits from the government."

"Sounds pretty cut and dry. How much?"

Pause. "Upwards of eight million."

Jolene whistled.

"My thoughts exactly."

"Have you told them my fee?"

"Of course. They asked for you specifically. You'll get your cut and…"

Here it was. She was expecting this.

"… and, as always, I get my percentage for finding you the gig. But I want more for this one. Twenty percent of your take."

"Dylan." Jolene narrowed her eyes. "Twenty percent?"

"Twenty percent."

She tapped the steering wheel, gazing at the dark house. "And if I say no?"

"I've got two other people who'd love to take it."

She gripped the wheel and a moment of silence slid by.

"Ten percent."

Silence.

"Ten percent or you can call one of your other guys who's bound to mess it up. I'm the best, Dylan, you know that."

"Fifteen percent."

"Ten."

"Dammit, Jolene. Deal."

"Good. I'm heading to New York tomorrow for an event; I'll give you a call and we'll meet up to discuss specifics."

"Sounds good."

Click.

Jolene shook her head. She liked to think she was a fair woman who understood the cost of business, but she didn't appreciate ultimatums. Fuck appreciate, she didn't tolerate it. And Dylan was always one to hustle her end of a deal.

Jolene had met Dylan not long after she'd arrived back in Texas, and for better or worse, Dylan was responsible for helping Jolene land her first job.

Fifteen years older than Jolene, Dylan was deep into the underground world of cybertheft, and over years, became somewhat of a manager to Jolene. Although the two women were like oil and water, they had built a professional respect for each other.

As Jolene began to make a name for herself, she set out on her own, but still maintained a working relationship with Dylan, who threw her jobs every now and again. Just like she was now.

Jolene got out of her car, hit the lock button and walked up the narrow sidewalk to the B&B. As she stepped onto the front porch, her instincts piqued immediately. Something wasn't right.

The house was dark with not a single light on, which was abnormal. Barb always left a few small lights on to make the house more warm and welcoming, she would say.

It was also quiet. Eerily so.

Where was Barb? Asleep?

She slid her key into the lock and opened the door. The hair on the back of her neck prickled as she stepped over the threshold. The air was still, heavy, and only the dim light from the outdoor lamp posts shone through the windows. She strained to listen to any noise; footsteps, or even the hum of the kitchen television Barb usually left on.

Silence.

Wide-eyed and alert, she slowly slid her hand into her purse and pulled out her Glock. Her compact, purse-size Glock, that she carried with her everywhere she went.

Holding it steady in her hand, she walked down the hallway, the old wood planks creaking underneath her as she glanced into each room. The house was pitch-black. A cool breeze brushed against her cheek as she stepped into the kitchen and saw the backdoor standing wide open.

Shit.

A break-in?

She raised her Glock, walked across the room and stepped outside into the darkness. The porch swing creaked back and forth in the breeze as she scanned the yard. Nothing out of the ordinary.

She turned, walked back into the house and closed the door behind her. Something still wasn't right.

"Barb?"

Silence.

She made her way to the front of the house and paused, looking at the staircase before cautiously taking the steps. With her gun raised, she climbed the staircase.

Tingles broke out over her body as she reached the second-floor landing. Yes, something was definitely wrong —her finely tuned sixth sense was now screaming at her.

Gripping her Glock, she scanned the hallway. The door to the unoccupied guest room was open, and the door to the young couple's room was closed. She stepped up to the closed door and pressed her ear against it. Nothing.

She knocked.

"Hello?"

Silence.

Her fingers slid around the brass doorknob, her other finger wrapped around the trigger of her gun as she slowly turned the knob and opened the door.

"Hello?"

A metallic scent filled her nose. A familiar smell that made her stomach sink.

Her heart began to pound.

"Hello?" A little louder.

She raised the gun, flicked on the light and scanned the room. Open suitcases on the floor, clothes strewn about. Crumpled sheets on the bed. Lube and a vibrator on the nightstand. Gross.

Her gaze landed on the closed bathroom door.

After taking a quick glance over her shoulder, she stealthily walked across the room and paused to listen.

"Hello?"

Nothing.

She slowly turned the knob. As the door creaked open, the beam from the bedroom light cut through the dark room. Her pulse spiked as she peered inside.

Fresh blood pooled on the tiled blue floor. Dark red spatters decorated the walls.

A bloodied leg hung over the bathtub.

She leapt into the bathroom, slipping on the blood-slicked tiles.

Breathless and bracing herself on the wall, she looked over the bathtub.

A young man… dead.

Her breath stopped.

Drained of all his blood, his pale skin matched the grey porcelain tub. Strands of his dark matted hair stuck to the side of the tub, looking like a black spider web spun from his head.

His right arm stretched above his head, his fingers delicately pointing at her. The other arm draped over his stomach, which was marked with multiple open wounds. A deep gash split the side of his face, his ear dangling by a thin pad of opaque skin.

His lifeless brown eyes looked up at her, expressionless and hollow with the finality of death.

She gasped.

She knew those eyes.

Chase.

Her stomach plummeted as she looked down at him, remembering their last encounter in the woods—the one with his gun pointed at her head.

CHAPTER 7

"ANNA?"

Jolene spun around on her heel, gun raised.

Barb gasped and threw her hands up in the air. Her wide eyes trailed from the gun to the bathtub. "Oh, my God! Who? What? *Oh, my God!*"

Heart racing, Jolene lowered the gun and slid it into the back of her pants. Breathless, she said, "Are you okay, Barb?"

The blood drained from Barb's face as she stepped into the gruesome bathroom. "Oh, my." She reached out her hand, bracing herself on the wall. "What happened?"

Jolene shook her head. "I don't know. I just got here and found him. Did you hear anything? See anyone?"

"Is it Mark? The gentleman staying here?"

"I'm…" Her mind raced. Should she say she knows him? No. Assess the situation, first. "No, I don't think so."

Just then, a gasp behind them.

"Oh, my *God!*"

Jolene turned around to see the young couple, Mark

and Tiffany, who were staying in the room. She slid her hand to her back, on the hilt of her gun.

Mark pushed Tiffany to the side. "What happened?" He stepped into the bathroom. "What the... who is this?" His voice pitched, eyes rounded. "Is he dead? Who is this? How...?"

"We need to get out of this room. Come on." Jolene guided Mark and Barb out of the bathroom, her eyes locked on the young couple, her head on a swivel.

Barb reached her unsteady hand toward Jolene. "I'm sorry, honey, I'm feeling lightheaded. Can you please help me sit down?"

Jolene eased Barb into a chair in the corner of the bedroom, and turned to Mark and Tiffany, who was as white as Tiffany's cotton shirt. She addressed Mark first.

"Do you know what happened here?"

Vehemently shaking his head, he said, "No. Absolutely not."

She looked around. "Where were you guys?"

Mark slid his girlfriend a glance. "We... um, we were in the room across the hall. We've been out, all evening, and just got back about thirty minutes ago."

"Why were you in the room across the hall?"

Tiffany looked down, her pale cheeks blushed.

"Um, we were in the bathroom," Mark answered.

"Why?"

"That room has a Jacuzzi, ours doesn't... we were... using it."

Jolene glanced down at his unbuttoned jeans and untied boots. She then looked at Tiffany, whose shirt was half unbuttoned. Ah. "Okay. Did you hear anything? See anyone?"

He shook his head.

She turned to Barb. "Barb, did you? See anyone? Anything?"

Breathless, Barb shook her head and said, "No. My God, no. I... I must've fallen asleep." She squeezed her eyes shut and shook her head. "I'm sorry... I'm not feeling well."

"Okay, let's get you downstairs and I'll make you some tea. And we need to call the police immediately."

Barb nodded. "Yes."

Panic flooded Mark's face. "Wait."

Jolene turned, narrowed her eyes.

"Oh, my God." He ran his fingers through his hair and began pacing. "There's a dead body in here! In the room that we're staying in! Won't they... won't they think it's us, maybe?"

Tiffany slapped him on the arm. "Don't say that!"

"Okay, guys calm down." Jolene walked up to Mark, her eyes leveled on his. "Calm down, Mark."

He took a deep breath. "Okay, okay. You're right. We have to call the cops."

"Come downstairs, we'll get this figured out."

Jolene followed the group downstairs, keeping her head on a swivel, and her hand on her gun. Dammit, the last thing in the world she needed was to be surrounded by law enforcement. She needed to start planning her exit strategy, STAT.

She eased Barb into a kitchen chair and grabbed her cell phone from her purse while Mark and Tiffany paced in the hallway.

"Nine-one-one, what's your emergency?"

"I'm at 418 Lake View Drive. There's a dead body in the house."

"Okay ma'am, are you in trouble?"

"I don't believe so."

"Is anyone else in the house?"

"Yes, the owner, and two guests."

"Where is the body?"

"In the second-floor bathroom."

"You're sure the person is deceased?"

Her stomach rolled. "Without question."

"What is your name?"

"Anna Gable."

"Okay, stay there, we're sending someone now."

Jolene slid her phone into her pocket and looked around. "Okay, guys, it's probably best if we wait outside and try to touch as little as possible."

Barb nodded. "Put some coffee on. It's going to be a long night."

The quiet night was shattered by the sound of the sirens screaming down the dirt road. Flashing lights lit up the dark night as an ambulance and two police cars pulled up to the B&B.

Jolene, Barb, Mark and Tiffany stood anxiously on the front porch.

Lights began flicking on in the few surrounding homes, followed by curious neighbors peering out their windows.

Chaos erupted as the medics and officers exited their vehicles. Jolene stood, bracing herself.

An officer jumped out of the second car, jogged across the street and onto the porch.

"Who's Anna Gable?"

"I am."

"Miss Gable, I'm Detective Jameson. Are you the one who called in the body?"

"Yes, sir."

"Where is it?"

"Upstairs in the bathroom. I think they, or whoever it was, got in through the back door. It was open when I got here."

He cut Barb a glance who was sitting in her rocking chair, dazed, sipping her coffee. "Ms. Barb, are you okay?"

Jolene wasn't surprised that the officer knew Barb. Everyone in town did.

"Hi, Eric. I think so. A little shaken up."

He looked at the two B&B guests, who were as white and wide-eyed as ghosts. "And you are?"

With nerves written all over his face, Mark stepped forward. "Mark Williams and this is Tiffany Lancaster."

Barb cut in. "They've been staying in the room the last two days."

"The room the victim was found in?"

"But we don't know him, sir."

Tiffany nodded enthusiastically. "That's right."

Jameson looked them over, allowing for the heavy weight of an awkward silence. He turned to Barb. "Ms. Barb, do you recognize the body?"

"No. Never seen him before in my life."

"Okay. Please stay outside while we search the house. I'll be back out in a bit to ask you all some more questions."

Jolene stepped aside as the medics jogged past her and another police car pulled up. Loud voices erupted from every direction and an officer was already busy securing the front yard with yellow police tape.

What a fucking night.

"Barb!"

Jolene turned to see Barb's neighbor, Mrs. Chapman, dressed in a pink robe and nightcap, step out on her porch. "Barb! Are you okay?" Her voice pitched and shaky, she hobbled across her lawn to the porch. "Are you in some kind of trouble?"

Barb shook her head. "No, Mrs. Chapman, I'm sorry about all the noise. Go back to bed."

"What's going on?"

"Nothing, really, please don't worry about it."

Her face drawn with concern, she said, "Okay, dear. You let me know if you need anything."

Jolene had only met Mrs. Chapman a few times but already knew two things about the woman. One, Jolene was ninety-nine percent sure that the nosy neighbor had a slight bout of dementia, and two, she loved to gossip. Jolene had no doubt that Mrs. Chapman would remember just enough to spread the gossip of the night's events to everyone in her phonebook by dawn.

As she watched Mrs. Chapman make her way across the lawn, she shook her head, then turned back to the house where shouts, muffled voices and banging echoed through the front door. Everything was happening so fast.

"What's happening, dear?"

Jolene glanced in the window. "A lot."

Pacing back and forth now, Barb shook her head. "I just can't believe this. I can't believe it. It's like a horror movie."

Yes, it was.

"Anna, run in there and grab me some Baileys for my coffee, and see if you can hear anything."

"They asked us to stay outside."

"It's my damn house. Just be quick. I want some liquor, and I want to know what's going on."

Truth be told, Jolene wanted to hear what the cops were saying, too. After a moment, she nodded and said, "Okay, I'll be right back."

Jolene slipped through the front door where Detective Jameson was busy dusting a white substance on the rails of the staircase. She briskly walked down the hall, into the kitchen, where an officer was speaking to a younger officer, who he called Willard, who was nodding enthusiastically. Donning latex gloves, both knelt down in front of the back door. White dust coated the door and the floor. Jolene stepped to the side and strained to listen.

"... and, look closely, here, at the top of the knob." The officer peered through a magnifying glass. "These look like fresh marks, from someone breaking in."

Officer Willard leaned closer. "A bump key?"

"Possibly. Of course, we'll need to ask Barb if the marks are from her."

Jolene grabbed the liquor bottle, walked back down the hall and glanced up at the staircase before stepping outside. The second floor was illuminated with the unforgiving glow of fluorescent lights. Quick flashes of light reflected from the bedroom, presumably from someone photographing the body.

She stepped outside, almost running full-force into a grumpy, balding man wearing a wrinkled button-up and a don't-mess-with-me look.

"Whoa, there."

Jolene stepped back. "Sorry."

The man glanced down at the liquor bottle glued to her hand, then back up. "You Anna Gable?"

She swallowed the lump in her throat. "Yes."

"I'm David McCord, chief of police."

"Hi."

"Did you call in the body?"

"Yes."

"Where's Barb?"

She nodded over her shoulder, where Barb had paced her way to the far side of the porch, and had her nose pressed to the window. Mark and Tiffany were huddled together on the porch swing, both still pale as ghosts.

"Ms. Barb, you okay?"

Barb peeled her face away from the window and bristled when she saw the police chief. "Yes, yes, I'm fine, Chief McCord."

"Okay." He slid a glance toward Jolene, then looked back at Barb. "Do you know Anna?"

"Yes, she's been renting the top unit from me for a month now."

"Okay." He looked at Anna. "Why don't you tell me how you found the body?"

Realizing her hand was still gripping the liquor bottle, she quickly set it on the chair and cleared her throat. "When I came inside...'

McCord interrupted. "Where were you before?"

"The next town over, browsing art shops."

"Okay, continue."

"Anyway, I didn't see Barb and something just seemed off."

"Off?"

"Yes."

He cocked his head, assessing her.

She continued, "So I checked around and as I made my way up to my apartment, I glanced through the bedrooms, and that's when I saw it."

"What compelled you to look through the rooms?"

She felt her defenses beginning to creep up. "As I said, I just felt like something was off."

"Why don't you elaborate on what you mean by *off* Miss Gable?"

She narrowed her eyes. "Off, as in, my instincts guided me. I assume you, being the chief of police, have been trained to recognize your finely-tuned instinct as a police officer."

He raised his eyebrows.

Barb stepped forward, sensing the potential sparing match. "And that's when I came in the room, right after she found him."

McCord peeled his icy gaze away from Jolene and looked at Barb. "And you said you were asleep before then?"

"Yes. I fell asleep watching television and woke up to get myself a glass of water when I heard someone in the vacant unit above me."

"Who?"

"The guests, they were using the Jacuzzi tub."

He looked over at Mark and Tiffany. "Them?"

Barb nodded.

"Do you know the victim?"

"No."

"Never seen him before?"

"No."

"Not familiar at all?"

Barb blew out a breath. "No, McCord, I've never seen the man before in my life."

He turned to Jolene. "You?"

"You what?"

"You know the victim?"

For a split-second, she hesitated. "No."

He looked back at Barb.

"Who has been in the house this evening?"

"Um, myself, Jolene, Mark and Tiffany, and that's it I think."

"Anyone else throughout the day?"

"Oh, um, Greg came by."

"Greg?"

"My cook. He cooks the guests' meals."

McCord scribbled in his notebook. "Who else do you have on staff?"

"No one. Just Greg and myself."

"Housekeeper?"

"You're looking at her."

He glanced at the front door. "Alright, ladies, I'll be back shortly and will have some more questions for you, and the guests. No one leave."

As McCord walked away, Barb shook her head.

"What?"

"Oh, McCord. Never did like him much. Has no people skills whatsoever."

"Yeah, I caught that."

Just then, Jameson stepped outside and shook his head. "Hell of a mess."

"Have you found anything yet?"

"Too early to say. The ME said the time of death looks to be around an hour ago."

"An hour ago?" Barb put her hand on her chest. "I can't believe it. While I was sleeping downstairs!"

A cool breeze swept up Jolene's back. "It looked like stab wounds?"

Jameson nodded. "That's the early presumption. How long were you gone?"

"Almost all day."

"Where to?"

"The next town over, browsing the art shops."

"They close around nine, right?"

"That's right. I grabbed a bite to eat before I headed home."

Jameson's inquisitive eyes narrowed.

She continued, "At the Fairy Garden. I'm sure you can pull the security cameras to verify."

He smiled. "I'm sure we will. Protocol, of course."

"Of course."

He glanced over Jolene's shoulder to the young couple on the porch swing. He lowered his voice and looked at Barb. "What do you know about those two?"

"Not much. They called last week and reserved the room for two nights. They're scheduled to leave tomorrow."

"They pay with cash, credit card?"

"Credit card."

"Do you know where they're from?"

She shook her head. "No, they've actually kept to themselves quite a bit. Been holed up in their room."

Jameson cocked his head. "The whole time?"

"Mostly."

"Do you know what they've been doing?"

"I have a pretty damn good guess based on the squeaking bed posts."

"Oh. Okay." He looked at the couple again. "I'll go interview them, and they'll have to find another place to stay tonight."

"What about their things?"

"We'll be analyzing every single thing in that room, Ms. Barb."

"Okay."

"Did McCord already question you ladies?"

Barb rolled her eyes and exhaled. "Yes, and I'm sure it won't be the last time."

"Are you not a fan of the chief, Barb?"

"Not since he hit on me when I first moved to town."

"And the plot thickens." Jameson glanced over his shoulder before saying. "He's good at his job. Hardass though. Don't let him push you around."

"I'm not in the habit of letting anyone push me around."

"I don't doubt that for a second. I'm going to go have a chat with your guests."

Jolene watched Jameson walk across the porch, and strained to listen.

"Mark and Tiffany, correct?"

Mark sat up, his back as straight as a rod. "Yes."

"Where are y'all from?"

"Birmingham. Sir."

"What are you doing in town?"

"Um, just passing through on the way to a friend's wedding."

Tiffany nodded, and barely taking a breath between words, she stuttered out, "And we heard this was a cute town with lots to do this time of year, so we decided to stop. Just for a few days… maybe do some hiking, maybe some fishing. Mark, um, he likes to fish. His dad taught him when he was really young. That's a funny story actually…"

Mark elbowed her. "Sorry, she talks a lot when she gets nervous."

She giggled, nervously. "Oh. Sorry."

"Why are you nervous, Tiffany?"

"Because… because someone was murdered in our room. Sir."

"And you said you don't recognize the victim?"

"No, sir."

"Where were you this evening?"

As Tiffany opened her mouth to speak, Mark cut her off. "We went out to eat and got back about thirty minutes before we saw it."

"Where did you eat?"

"A diner, on the square."

"You didn't go to your room when you got back?"

"No, we went to the room across the hall."

"In another guest's room?"

"No one was staying in it. We just wanted to use the Jacuzzi."

Jameson cleared his throat. "Alright. And how long did you use the bath?"

"About thirty minutes."

Tiffany looked down, her face beet red.

"Did you leave your room unattended today?"

"Just to get lunch and dinner."

"Did you leave the house?"

"Not for lunch. The cook… Greg, I think it is, makes delicious meals."

"Did you see anyone on the second floor before you went into the other guest room?"

"No."

"Hear anything at all?"

"No, but the Jacuzzi was loud, and we had music playing, too."

"And to confirm, you do not know the victim?"

"No. No, sir."

"*Jameson.*" Jameson turned toward the front door where an officer was yelling his name. "I'll be right there." He turned back to Mark and Tiffany. "I've got to run inside, but we need you to come to the station for an official statement. You'll need to find another place to stay tonight."

"Okay."

As Jameson made his way across the porch, Barb grabbed his arm. "Did you get any information out of them?"

"A little." He placed a hand on Barb's shoulder. "We'll get this figured out, okay?" He gave Barb a sympathetic look before disappearing into the house.

Jolene took a deep breath and leaned against the railing.

It was going to be a long night.

CHAPTER 8

JAMESON CLICKED ON his flashlight and stepped onto the narrow, rock trail that stretched a few yards from the back of the B&B, to the lake. Barb kept the trail clean and well-manicured for her guests to enjoy the area.

The buzz of the commotion behind him began to fade as he neared the lake. The smell of water scented the air and the sound of waves lapping against the shore told him he was close. He scanned the trail with his flashlight, looking for any trace of recent activity, or any evidence whatsoever.

A rustle of leaves had his head snapping to the side. He shone his light, and placed his other hand firmly on the gun in his waistband.

Just a squirrel.

Damn, it was a dark night.

He pressed on until the lake, which looked like a large black mass, finally came into view. He paused to look around and listen, before stepping onto the dock.

Both Barb's fishing boats—frequently used by guests—

were tightly secured to the dock and swayed back and forth in the dark water.

It was a covered dock, with a small equipment room off to the side. He flashed his light along the roof of the dock and then along the sides. No footprints or sign that anyone had been there recently. He walked over to the equipment room and peered inside. Life jackets, cleaning supplies, nothing out of the ordinary. The door was securely locked.

After taking one more look around, he stepped off the dock and scanned the shoreline. No footprints.

He turned, gazed into the dark woods and something deep inside told him that this was going to be a hell of a case.

❧

Ethan pushed through the front doors of Frank's Bar, and was welcomed by the permeating smell of smoked meats and beer. He glanced at the rusted clock on the wall, almost eleven o'clock in the evening.

He'd spent the day fishing and the evening working on the cabin, and was more than ready for a beer with the guys.

From across the room a hand shot up, motioning to him.

"Hey, Ethan."

"Hey, guys." Ethan took a glance around the table where Eric Jameson, Dean Walker and a guy he didn't recognize sat around a pitcher of beer. He tossed his cell phone on the table and sat down.

"Did you ever meet Jonas when you were in town?"

"Don't think so."

"Well, Ethan, this is Jonas, our Evidence Tech slash Information Specialist slash unofficial Forensic Analyst at the station—he kind of does it all—and Jonas, this is Ethan Veech. He's with the Cyber Crimes Unit at the FBI."

Jonas's blue eyes widened. "No shit?"

"No shit."

Jonas slid a glance from side to side. "Something going on that I don't know about?"

Ethan laughed. "No, I'm just here on vacation."

Dean motioned to the waitress before saying, "You remember that anti-government group we busted a month ago? He came down for that."

Ethan raised his eyebrows. "*You* busted?"

"Damn straight."

Ethan laughed, and considering the company he was in, decided against reminding Dean that the local PD was a consistent step behind the FBI in the last Berry Springs case.

"What can I git ya?" The waitress, clad in a red plaid shirt, black leather skirt, and cowboy boots popped her gum while eyeing the newcomer.

"A beer, ma'am."

"You got it."

Jameson sipped his beer and leaned back. "Here's to hoping we don't have another sticky case on our hands."

"What do you mean?"

He slid a look at Dean before saying, "There was a murder at the local B&B earlier this evening."

"A murder? No kidding?"

"No kidding. A man stabbed to death."

"Any relation to the bones that were just pulled from the lake?"

"Doubt it." Jameson paused, contemplated. "Hell, maybe. Can't rule that out, yet."

"What do you know?"

"His name was Chase Martinez. Age thirty-two, single, no kids, waiter, born and raised in Florida."

"Here you go." The waitress slid an ice-cold beer in front of Ethan.

"Thanks." He sipped and sat back, his analytical mind already dissecting the dead body.

Dean showed him a picture from his phone. "Ring any bells?"

Ethan peered at the picture of a young man leaning back in a pick-up truck, gazing intimidatingly into the camera. The picture was obviously a selfie that he must have posted to social media.

Ethan shook his head. "No, not familiar."

"Apparently, not many people know him either. He has no next of kin—both parents deceased—and no siblings. We ID'd him through the driver's license found in his pocket and his social media account. Got a rap sheet—a few B&E's, theft."

"Interesting. Any suspects yet?"

"I don't think we can officially label them suspects yet, but a Mr. Mark Williams and Miss. Tiffany Lancaster were staying in the room where it happened. Out-of-towners."

"They were *in* the room?"

"According to their story, no. They'd just gotten back from dinner and were banging in the Jacuzzi tub in the next room over."

Ethan raised his eyebrows. "Assuming no alibi for that, right?"

"Right."

"What about for dinner?"

"Yeah, they went to the diner. On camera."

"No cameras inside in the B&B?"

Jameson laughed. "No, not in Barb's B&B. She comes from a time when people left their doors unlocked all the time. There's one out front, but it was turned off."

"What do you know about them?"

"They're a new couple, passing through town to a friend's wedding. Making a little vacation out of it. They're from Birmingham; salesman and an office manager."

"Any link to the victim, Chase?"

"Not yet, but we've just begun digging. We've got them staying at the Motel Eight tonight and are hoping to question them again tomorrow morning again before they go."

"Hoping?"

"They lawyered up real damn fast."

"What does your gut tell you?"

"Innocent. Looks like someone broke in through the back door."

Ethan chewed on his lower lip. "You said the dude had a wallet on him. Anything interesting in it?"

"Just his Florida license and a few credit cards. We're running those transactions now to see if there's anything suspicious. The wallet's at the lab now, being analyzed."

"Does he have a residence in Florida?"

Jameson nodded. "An apartment. McCord's already called the local PD; they're probably there now."

"Phone?"

He shook his head. "Nope."

"Car?"

"Nope. Not outside the B&B at least."

"Florida, huh? What's he doing in Berry Springs, I wonder."

"We've got some of the rookies calling around to the local motels, car rentals, etcetera to see if we can find out where he was staying. He had to get here somehow, and he had to stay somewhere. Someone knows something."

Ethan nodded.

Jonas reached for the pitcher and poured himself another drink. "Any significant evidence at the scene?"

"We bagged up the entire bathroom, and will send it off for analysis."

Jonas snorted. "They'll be chasing their tails. Do you know how much DNA is in a hotel room?"

"Yeah, tons, and hopefully a little of whoever the hell did this."

Ethan sipped his drink. "Anything else?"

Jameson nodded. "First thing we noticed was that there were shoe prints smeared in the blood on the floor. We're assuming most of those belong to Barb and the girl who found the body, but they're running analysis on them."

"What about bloody prints leading out of the bathroom? The killer had to leave, right?"

Jameson nodded. "Unfortunately, at least two other people did too. So their tracks are mixed with his, or hers. But the killer was careful. Very careful. There's no tracks leading to the back door."

Dean spun his beer on top of the table. "They'll run a BPA on the blood spatters on the walls, too. They'll search for any DNA whatsoever on the items in the bathroom. Something will turn up."

"What about DNA on him? Chase's body?"

"McCord will try to push the autopsy through quickly, but they're backed up, like always. Once he receives the full report, it will tell us a lot. Hopefully Chase will have DNA under his nails, or somewhere, from where he defended himself."

"And I'm assuming no murder weapon was found."

"Nope. We've got rookie Willard searching the trash cans, dumpsters, you name it."

"So really you guys have jack shit right now."

"Tests and analysis take time."

Dean nodded. "Until then, we'll work our asses off to figure out where Chase was, who he talked to and what he was doing the forty-eight hours leading up to his death."

"And why the hell he was in Berry Springs."

"Exactly."

Ethan flicked the bottle cap that Dean was aimlessly spinning between his fingers, across the table, to which Dean responded by grabbing Ethan's unopened beer, popping the top and downing half the contents.

Dean grinned and wiped his mouth. "Thanks." And he began spinning the new bottle cap on the table.

Ethan smirked, then looked back at Jameson. "What about the owner of the B&B? She clear?"

"Barb?" Jameson laughed. "Hell, yes, she pushing sixty, and been here for over twenty years. That woman wouldn't hurt a fly."

"You said something about a girl finding him?"

Jameson's eyes narrowed as he scratched his head. "Yeah, so we're looking into that."

"Into what? Who?"

"Her name is Anna. Been renting the top apartment from Barb for a month."

A surge of electricity shot up Ethan's spine. "Did you say Anna?"

"Yeah." Jameson raised his eyebrows. "And let me tell you something, chick is not bad to look at."

Dean tipped up his beer. "He's not joking."

Ethan tried to hide his interest by casually leaning back in his chair. "What did she say?"

"Just that she had been out for the day, returned and found the body."

"Did you verify her story?"

"Of course. She was eating dinner, solo, at The Fairy Garden in the timeframe we believe Chase was murdered."

Ethan tapped his beer, in deep thought. "What do you know about her?"

"Not much, yet."

Dean leaned forward. "But bottom line, we've verified her whereabouts during the murder."

Jonas nodded. "Don't waste your time on her." He grinned. "I'm planning to do that."

Jameson laughed. "You gonna make a move?"

Jonas shrugged. "Why not?"

Dean clicked his glass. "Go for it, man."

Ethan's wheels began spinning a mile a minute. He'd only just recently realized that Anna Gable was none other than Jolene Reeves, under surveillance by the FBI, and now, she was responsible for finding a dead body. Coincidence? He had to find out.

"So are they still staying at the B&B or did you evict them while you scanned the house?"

Jameson shook his head. "No, we let Anna and Barb stay and just blocked off the second floor, where the body was found. There's three floors and a basement—the basement is where Barb lives and the third floor is Anna's apartment. There's one unit on the first floor, and two on the second."

"I see." He started to ask another question when his phone dinged, alerting him of a text message. Ethan looked down at the text, but before he could pick it up, Jameson snatched it away.

"Debbie?" Jameson looked around the table. "As in *Diner Debbie?*"

Ethan grabbed his phone as Jonas pounced. "You guys hooking up?"

Dean raised his eyebrows. "Damn, you move fast, bro. Haven't you only been here forty-eight hours?"

Ethan rolled his eyes and turned off his phone. "Relax. No, we're not *hooking up.*"

"Well, what did she want, then?"

"She wants to take me to some barbecue place while I'm in town."

Jameson cocked an eyebrow. "Barbecue, huh?"

"As in, a date?"

Ethan shook his head. "Hate to disappoint you guys, but it's just dinner."

Jonas snorted. "Yeah, right."

"You guys seriously think I'd try to get into a relationship in my five days here?"

"Not many men can deny our very own little miss Diner Debbie."

"So I've heard."

Jameson clinked his beer. "Let us know how it goes."

∽

"Good night, Barb. Are you sure you don't need anything else?"

"No, dear, it's past eleven o'clock, go home, get some sleep. Thanks for coming by to check on me. I'm going to turn on the "No Vacancy" sign for a while, or at least until this mess gets figured out." She took a deep breath. "So I won't need you to cook for a while."

Greg nodded. Vacation. Nice. "Okay Barb. You call me if you need anything."

"Will do, dear."

He grabbed his jacket from the coat rack and pushed out the back door. The cool wind whipped around him as he jumped into his truck.

Dammit, he missed summer already.

He vigorously rubbed his hands together to fight off the cold before starting the ignition and backing away from the B&B.

A smirk slid over his face. As much as he enjoyed Barb and cooking at the B&B, he sure as hell wouldn't mind a few days off.

He inhaled. A few days just to himself, to do whatever the hell he wanted. What to do? What to do?

Debbie.

That's what he would like to do.

His stomach sank. He hadn't talked to her since that night. Since that utterly humiliating, embarrassing, godforsaken night. He'd been relentlessly checking his phone, in hopes she would call or text. But she hadn't. And neither had he. He'd started to, about a million times, but stopped. He'd written up the same 'I'm sorry for making you feel uncomfortable' text over and over again, but could never hit the send button. Why? He wasn't sure. Maybe he was just hoping the embarrassing moment would fade away, like everything else in his damn life.

He flicked on his headlights and pulled onto the dirt road. The abnormally cool fall evening had the town staying indoors, mentally preparing for the cold winter to come. He rolled to a stop at the four-way and hesitated. Should he?

Yes.

He flicked his turn signal and made a left. Fifteen minutes later, he turned onto Main Street and spotted her car and a rush of excitement flooded his veins. He knew she'd be working, but it still excited him just to be close to her.

Slowly, he pulled into a parking spot across from Donny's Diner and turned off the engine. The cab of his truck went dark and he gazed into the windows. This was the best spot for watching her work; he'd learned that long ago.

There she was. Oh, God. In a low-cut blouse, mopping the floors, getting ready to go home for the evening, he assumed.

God, she was sexy.

He leaned his head back and watched from behind the darkness of his windshield.

He watched her thighs sway from side-to-side as she walked back and forth to the kitchen. He watched the cleavage spill from her shirt as she bent over, wiping tables.

He watched her smile and laugh with the manager. Flirting, of course.

His thoughts trailed to their last night together. To her breasts, her nipples, her wetness.

His pulse picked up as his pants began to tighten.

Glancing from side-to-side to confirm no one was watching him—watching her—he slid his hand below the steering wheel and onto his jeans. The touch almost made him jump.

He was so turned on just seeing her.

He took one more glance in the rearview mirror before unzipping his jeans.

Sweat began to bead on his forehead as he stroked back and forth. His breath became shallow as he watched her bend over and wipe down a table, her breasts calling out to him.

He tightened his grip and stroked harder, faster, until the tip began to tingle.

She looked up.

Right at him.

Oh, my God.

He tore his hand away, quickly zipped up, and pretended like he was changing stations on the radio. Yeah, just sitting in the cold, with the engine off, clicking in between radio stations. *Dammit.*

He looked up to see her sauntering across the sidewalk. Oh, no.

He shifted in his seat, attempting to hide all evidence of his lust, and rolled down the window.

"Hey, Greg." A forced smile barely crossed her lips.

"Uh, hey."

She glanced back at the diner. "We're closed, you know."

He cleared his throat. "Oh, uh, no I'm just waiting on Paul. We're meeting here and then gonna hit the bars."

"Oh." She paused, eyeing him. "Okay." Her phone rang. "I've gotta take this. Have a good night." She hesitated. "Good to see you."

"You, too."

She pressed the phone to her ear and stepped up on the sidewalk.

"Hello? Hey, girl... Yeah, I'm working tonight... I wish! Yeah, I just texted him. Believe me I'd rather be on a date with him right now than working in this damn diner. He's so freakin' hot... No, not yet... I know... Ethan... Veech, I think... Alright girl, sounds good. Talk later."

His stomach churned as he watched her click off the phone and walk back into the diner.

She was going on a date? With someone other than him? What the fuck! They'd just had sex, and she was already making a date with someone else? What the fuck? And who the fuck?

Ethan Veech.

Ethan. Veech.

CHAPTER 9

ETHAN ROLLED TO a stop at the four-way, and hesitated. He looked in his rearview mirror, then from left to right—not a car in sight. Not that it was surprising considering it was almost midnight and the whole town shut down at nine. Except for Frank's Bar, of course.

He squinted to see ahead, his headlights barely illuminating the B&B sign at the end of the road.

What was he going to do? Knock on the door and say, *Hey, I know who you are?*

He ran his fingers through his hair.

No.

Maybe he'd just small-talk before going in for the kill. Yes, that makes more sense.

He took a deep breath. He needed to think of something, quick, because he knew Jolene was a flight risk. He couldn't lose her.

Anna, *or Jolene*, was under surveillance by the government and now she was responsible for finding a dead body in the same building where she lived. Coincidence? Maybe. Maybe not. Regardless, it was only a matter of time before local PD uncovered her real identity and turned her over to the FBI. They would turn her over without giving him a chance to question her first, and he wouldn't get the pat on the back for finding her.

Yep, being the one to find Jolene Reeves would be a feather in his cap.

Okay, so now what?

His fingers nervously tapped the steering wheel. Maybe he'd just do a slow drive-by to see if a light was on… and then just go from there.

Good idea.

He released the brake, slowly pressed the accelerator and took one more glance in the rearview mirror.

WHACK!

His stomach plummeted as he looked forward and saw a body tumble to the street.

"*Oh, shit!*"

He shoved the car into park, flung the door open and leapt to the front of his truck.

He fell to his knees. "Oh, my God, are you okay?"

The woman, dressed in jogging gear, groaned, rolled onto her side, and pushed up to her knees.

Ethan grabbed her hand. "Are you okay?"

She looked up, and he looked at her. *Jolene.* Holy shit, he just ran over Jolene.

Recognition flickered in her eyes before she looked down again.

"Bull's-eye. You got me."

He grinned and relief flooded him. If she was cracking a joke, she was okay. Thank God.

"Are you sure you're okay?"

"Yes."

"Here, let me help you up."

She winced as she stood, and Ethan glanced down at her knee, wet with blood.

"Dammit, your knee."

She shifted her weight and shook her head. "Oh, that's nothing compared to my face."

"Your face?" Ethan tilted her chin up and turned her head. Sure enough, there was a bump about the size of a quarter already forming on her upper cheek.

Son of a bitch!

He felt *terrible*. He softly ran his finger over the bump. "I'm so, so sorry. Gonna be a hell of a shiner."

"Not my first."

"Here, let me look into your eyes."

She cocked a brow.

"You might have a concussion."

She turned her face toward him and his finger lingered on her chin a moment too long. She looked up at him, her whiskey brown eyes sparkling under the moonlight. She was so beautiful. Time seemed to stop. The world went silent. And for a moment, as he gazed into her spellbinding eyes, he forgot what he was doing, where he was, or hell, his own name.

He suddenly became aware that he was still holding her hand, but before he could react, she looked down and pulled away.

"I'm sure I'm fine."

He stuttered. "Okay. Um, again, I'm so sorry." He looked down at her knee. "Can I give you a ride home?"

She glanced down the road. "I actually live just down there. I'll be fine."

"I insist."

She glanced down at her knee, then nodded. "Sure. Alright."

He noticed her biting her lip as she tried to hide her limp, and her pain, as she walked to the side of his truck. He opened the door and eased her inside.

He'd just hit damn Jolene Reeves.

He blew out a breath and jumped in the driver's seat.

᙭

About eight seconds later, the truck stopped in front Barb's B&B.

"Can I help you clean up?"

She shot him a look.

He shook his head. "Dammit, sorry, that came out wrong." He cleared his throat. "I meant, your knee."

"I'll be fine."

"It's the least I can do. Besides, I'd feel awful if I saw on the news tomorrow morning, *Woman slips into a coma after idiot runs over her with his truck.*"

She smirked. "Idiot? I can think of a more fitting name than that."

He laughed, his eyes twinkling in the moonlight. Did he remember meeting her the other night? She definitely remembered him. Instantly. The moment she saw him through the smudged windshield, right before he nailed her with his damn truck.

He was taller than she remembered, and even more muscular.

She'd slipped into Frank's Bar that night for a quick drink, just to get out of her apartment, without any intention of being social, or meeting someone of the opposite sex. But she had and here he was again. Looking at her from the driver's seat of his truck.

He was strikingly handsome, in a rugged woodsman kind of way. He carried an undeniable presence. A strong, male presence. The kind that always made her look twice.

Before she could make up an excuse for not allowing him inside, he turned off the engine, jumped out, and opened her door.

He reached out his hand. She gripped, and he lightly pulled her to her feet.

"I'm fine, really."

He looked down at her. "I insist."

She looked at the dark house, contemplating, and then back at him. "We'll have to be quiet, I'm sure Barb is asleep."

He smiled and helped her out of the truck. Her knee ached as she put weight on it.

They stepped onto the sidewalk.

"Who's Barb?"

"The owner of the B&B, my landlord. She's a pistol."

Her eyes landed on a piece of "*do not cross*" police tape tangled in a bush, blowing in the breeze. All of the police tape had already been taken down, but apparently this one got caught in the wind.

"I heard about the… body." He glanced at her. "How you holdin' up?"

She frowned. "I don't know… it's hard to get the image out of my head, to be honest."

He walked next to her up the sidewalk. Close enough to catch her if she fell, but not so close to feel intrusive.

"I bet. I heard it was pretty brutal. You found him right?"

She nodded.

"Must've been rough walking in on that. Do you know the couple that was staying in the room?"

She looked at him. "How do you know all this?"

"I'm friendly with the local cops."

Okay, so she'd need to watch her step with this one. She changed the subject. "Are you from here?"

"No. DC."

They reached the steps to the front porch, and as she began to raise her leg, pain shot through her knee.

Ethan grabbed her arm. "You okay?"

She grit her teeth. "Yes."

"No, you're not."

In one swift movement, he bent over, swept her off her feet, and carried her up the steps.

Before she could respond, he carefully set her back down.

She looked at him and cocked an eyebrow. "Well, I don't know how they do things in DC, but where I'm from, a guy might get his face slapped for that little maneuver."

"Good thing I'm not from where you're from. By the way, where are you from?"

"You already asked me that, remember?"

He grinned. "So you do remember meeting me the other night."

"How could I forget? I still have the hundred bucks."

"And here I thought it was my winning smile."

"You mean losing." She winked.

A blinking light caught his eye and he looked above the door. "Security camera?"

"Yep, only one." She glanced up. "I guess it's working now. Our cook, Greg, suggested that Barb put it up. She doesn't even know how to use it."

"Good security is important."

She unlocked and opened the front door. The house was dark, with only the low glow of a table lamp lighting their way.

"Well, good evening." Barb stepped out of the kitchen.

"Hi, Barb, I'm sorry, were we too loud?"

"No, not at all." She walked down the hall and extended her hand toward Ethan. "Barb."

They shook hands. "Ethan Veech."

"Pleasure to meet you, Mr. Veech." She winked at Jolene. "Alright then, I'll leave you two alone. I was on my way to bed anyway."

"Good night, Ms. Barb."

"Night."

As Barb headed downstairs, Ethan turned toward Jolene. "Where's the kitchen?"

"First you run over me and then you want me to make you a late-night snack?"

He laughed and glanced down the hall. "Ah, it's straight ahead. Come on."

She rolled her eyes and followed him.

"Sit." He walked to the refrigerator as she gladly took the weight off her knee and folded into the kitchen chair. A second later, he returned with a wrapped, raw steak.

"Steak?"

He leaned over, lightly tilted her chin up, and placed the ice-cold meat on her eye.

"Here, hold it there, okay? It will help with the swelling." He leaned up and looked down at her. "Now, where's the first-aid kit in this place?"

"There's one under the sink in the bathroom, just down the hall."

She watched him walk down the hall, his plain white T-shirt hanging tightly against his broad shoulders and muscular back. Her eyes drifted down to his backside where his jeans fit neither too tight or too loosely around his perfectly formed ass.

Despite the ice on her face, she felt her cheeks begin to heat, and she shook her head.

Get a grip, Jolene.

He returned a second later, scooted a chair over, sat down, and guided her leg onto his lap. She watched his every move as he opened the bottle of hydrogen peroxide and dabbed a cotton ball. With surprising tenderness, he began wiping her wound.

Keeping his eyes on her knee, he said, "I really am sorry."

"Yeah, me too."

He looked up and smiled, his hazel eyes lingering on hers for a brief moment before looking back down. "What were you doing out so late?"

"Late is relative. I was out jogging."

"Into cars."

"Oh, no, no, no, *you* hit *me*. You were at a full stop when I started across the road."

"I know, you're right. Do you always go for a jog at midnight?"

"Sometimes. When I can't sleep."

"I don't know many girls who jog in the middle of the night."

"I don't know many boys who run them over."

He grinned and unwrapped a fairy princess band-aid. "So you go to bars alone, drink Jack and Coke, know plenty about African mammals, and jog in the middle of the night."

"Intrigued?"

His eyes met hers with an intensity that made her heart skip a beat. "More than you know."

He lightly applied the bandage, guided her leg back to the floor and leaned forward on his elbows.

"You said your name was Anna, right?"

She nodded and nerves knotted her stomach.

"Anna Gable?"

Another nod.

He narrowed his eyes. "Where are you from, Anna Gable?"

Her pulse picked up. She hesitated, then said, "Texas."

Something flashed in his eyes.

She instinctively pulled back. Their flirty banter was suddenly replaced with an intensity that weighed down the room.

She cleared her throat. "Well, thanks for fixing me up."

His eyes remained locked on hers as he slowly nodded.

Her senses piqued. Something wasn't right. She stood. "I'll show you out."

He followed her down the hall onto the front porch. The night had darkened since they'd been inside, the cool breeze halted.

"Have a good night, Ethan."

He turned and she saw his lip curve up. "You remembered my name."

"Yes."

A thick cloud drifted over the moon covering his face in shadows.

His voice lowered, "I remember yours, too."

Her pulse picked up as she searched his face for any emotion, but could only see the dark outline of his tall, muscular body. Her hand searched for the doorknob behind her as he said...

"Jolene."

CHAPTER 10

LIKE A FLASH of lightning, she turned on her heel and bolted into the house. Ethan leapt after her, bouncing off the front door as she slung it closed behind her.

He pushed through the door just in time to see the back door slap closed.

"Dammit!"

He darted down the hall, through the back door and saw Jolene's slim figure sprint through the backyard.

He took off like a rocket after her, down the dirt road and into the woods. Dark shadows from the trees blackened around him as twigs and branches slapped at his clothes.

Damn, she was fast.

Like a gazelle.

The cold air burned his lungs as he pushed on, wondering where the hell she was going. Finally, the heavy clouds drifted and the woods were illuminated by the moon.

There she was, headed straight for the lake.

Okay, enough of this bullshit. He grit his teeth and pushed harder, gaining on her with every step. He was so close, he could smell her perfume.

"Jolene, *stop*."

They burst through the tree line, onto the shoreline. She jumped over a fallen tree branch and stumbled on the landing. Before she could catch herself, he slammed his body into hers.

They tumbled to the ground.

"*Ow*! Dammit! *Damn you*!"

Ethan rolled on top of her and pinned her to the ground. His fingers wrapped around her wrists and sank into the wet sand. A cold wave of water washed underneath them. Chest heaving, he looked down at her, her eyes piercing daggers through him.

"Let me go."

He gripped tighter and shook his head. "Oh, *hell, no.* Not after that little chase."

She narrowed her eyes and glared at him. "Who the hell are you?"

"Ethan Veech, FBI."

She shook her head. "I should've known." Her eyes widened. "Wait a second, did you *intentionally* run me over?"

"No. That was an honest accident."

She narrowed her eyes.

"Seriously, it was an accident. I swear."

"What? No Drivers' Ed at the Academy?"

He raised his eyebrows. "You've got quite the attitude, you know that?"

Another glare.

He took another deep breath, looked at the dark lake, then back down at her. "Jolene Reeves."

She sighed.

"Am I right?"

"You're FBI, you should know."

"You seriously couldn't think of a better name than Anna Gable?"

She almost grinned. Almost.

"You pulled a gun on my buddy, Jake, you know."

"I can neither confirm nor deny that."

"Maybe not. But the state capitol building surveillance camera can."

She looked away for a moment. "So what? Are you arresting me now?"

Still straddling her with his hands wrapped around her wrists, he leaned down, inches from her face. A swift breeze blew through the trees allowing for the silver beams of moonlight to dance across her face. He felt her breath on his skin as he looked into her eyes, twinkling in the moonlight.

In a low, husky voice he said, "I want something else from you."

She raised her eyebrows.

"I want your help."

"My help?"

He nodded.

"My help with what, exactly?"

"Your help bringing down Slade Packer."

"Well, what do you think?"

Seated comfortably behind the two-way mirror, McCord kept his eyes leveled on Mark Williams, whose pale skin matched the white paint in the interview room.

"Besides the fact that he looks like he's about to barf all

over the table? I think we've got about five more minutes until Perry breaks up the party."

Jameson nodded. "Agreed."

Just then, *knock, knock, knock.*

McCord rolled his eyes before opening the door.

Clyde Perry, Berry Springs's only lawyer, leaned against the doorframe. "Times up, boys. My clients have been more than gracious with their time."

McCord stood. "Perry, it's always such a pleasure."

Perry grinned. It was widely known that the police chief and small-town lawyer had a tumultuous relationship, to say the least.

Jameson stood. "Perry, come on, man, we've got a dead body in the room where they were staying, and we've confirmed they were in the building at the time of the murder. And they have no alibi. Give us some more damn time."

"That's incorrect, Jameson. We have them on camera entering the diner during the presumed time of the murder."

"Until Jessica completes the autopsy, we don't have a presumed time of murder."

Perry shook his head. "Nope, no more time Jameson. Not only have you two succeeded in scaring the shit out of them, you have absolutely nothing concrete to hold them for."

"Why the hell was the body in *their* room, Perry? There's got to be a connection somewhere. Can you at least wait until we get the DNA scan back from the autopsy?"

Perry shook his head, again. "No. Mark and Tiffany are ready to get the hell out of Berry Springs."

McCord blew out a breath and pushed past him. "Like I said, always a fucking pleasure, Perry."

Jameson grabbed his notebook as Perry patted him on the back. "Don't know how the hell you work with that guy."

"Somedays, neither do I." He glanced over Clyde's shoulder. "Gotta run." He stepped past the lawyer and jogged down the hall. "Hey, Dean."

Dean stopped mid-stride.

"You busy?"

"Always."

"Walk with me to my office."

Dean looked past Jameson, met eyes with Perry and then grinned. "Ah, I see. He's cut our suspects loose, hasn't he?"

"He always does." They fell in step together, walking through the bullpen. Chatter, ringing phones, and cuss words echoed around them.

"Any updates?"

"I checked on the autopsy first thing this morning. As expected, it's not done yet, but should be soon."

"Define soon."

"Jessica said possibly by the end of the day, but probably tomorrow."

"Alright. Keep at it. What else have you dug up about our victim?"

"Not a lot. I called some of his friends that we found on his social media page. Interviewed them, but from what I can tell, Chase Martinez was a loner. Only had two significant friends, really, and both said he'd become very elusive the last six months or so and that they hadn't talked to him."

"Elusive?"

"Yeah, just stopped calling and hanging around them." Dean followed Jameson into his office. "This dude was a major loner. Oh, and he traveled a lot."

"Traveled? How do you know that?"

Dean grinned. "I already got the warrant pushed through to access his credit cards."

"Damn you're good. Okay, where'd he travel to?"

"I haven't scanned all of the cards yet, but New York City seems to be the most frequent."

Jameson cocked an eyebrow. "Florida to New York City on a waiter's salary? Must get some nice tips."

"Yeah, there's got to be another source of money somewhere."

"Exactly. Girlfriend?"

"Not that his buddies knew of and no signs on social media or email."

"Surely he was hanging out with someone. What about work associates?"

Dean shook his head. "Nope, he would come into work—The Eggplant Café—and go home right afterward. Oh, they did find a laptop at his apartment and it's at the lab now."

Jameson grabbed two Cokes out of his mini fridge and tossed one to Dean. He popped the top and sank into his desk chair. Gazing at the ceiling he said, "All we know right now is that it appears that one of three things happened to Mr. Chase Martinez. One, Mark Williams and Tiffany Lancaster murdered him in their room. Or, two, Chase broke into Barb's B&B and murdered himself for no apparent reason. Or, three, someone broke into Barb's B&B, presumably with Mr. Martinez, marched him upstairs to the second floor unit, stabbed him to death and threw him in the bathtub."

Dean slowly nodded. "Theory one *seems* the most plausible."

Jameson took a deep sip of his Coke. "Maybe, but it doesn't explain the back door break-in."

"So they assume they were in the building during the time of the murder... they said they were across the hall banging in the Jacuzzi, right?"

"Right."

"The bathtub was wet, right?"

"Yep. But they could have staged the scene, of course."

"Let's assume they didn't stage the scene and they were really going at it in the tub..."

Jameson interrupted. "Because that's what you'd like to imagine, you sick son of a bitch."

Dean laughed, "No, I don't have to imagine banging in a Jacuzzi; I have one of my own."

Jameson laughed, "Alright, alright, alright, I don't need to know about your extracurricular activities. What were you saying?"

"Before I was rudely interrupted? I was saying; let's assume they were banging in the tub. Why the hell wouldn't they have heard the screams of someone being stabbed to death?"

"I thought the same thing. But the radio was left on in the bathroom, on the *slow* jams station nonetheless, and the Jacuzzi makes a good amount of noise when it's running."

"Making all those bubbles."

"Right, you sicko."

"So you don't think they could hear someone screaming?"

"Maybe. Maybe not."

In deep thought, Dean gazed out the window, then said, "Still no info back on the bones found in the lake."

Pause. "Do you think it's related?"

"I sure as hell hope not."

CHAPTER 11

THE EARLY MORNING beams of sunlight sliced through her windshield as she bumped along the dirt road. She glanced at the crumpled-up napkin in the passenger seat—341 County Road 3228. Well, she knew she was on the right road, but she hadn't passed a house for what seemed like miles.

Finally, up ahead, a mailbox. She slowed, rolled the window down. 341. She looked up the steep rock driveway and hesitated, her fingers tightening around the steering wheel.

Should she do it?

Did she have a choice? Nope. He'd made sure of that last night.

She rolled her eyes and blew out a breath.

Dammit.

As she reached the top of the driveway, the rock and log cabin came into view. Dead leaves danced across the wrap-around porch. A porch swing swayed in the breeze. Smoke drifted out of the chimney. She cocked her head—a *tilted* chimney.

She turned off the engine and glanced at her watch. Eight o'clock. Why the hell did he want to meet so early?

Ignoring the pit in her stomach, she got out of the car, walked up the porch steps and knocked on the door. From inside she heard the muted tones of classic rock blaring from somewhere in the house.

She knocked again.

Nothing.

"Oh, give me a break," she said under her breath as she knocked one more time before turning the knob. The door popped open and a solo guitar riff vibrated through the air as she stepped inside.

"Hello?"

Nothing.

"I said, *hello*."

Annoyed, she slapped the door closed behind her and walked down the hall, peering into each room. She stepped into the kitchen and a cold gust of air swept over her skin, from an open window. A radio was propped up against the frame.

She walked to the back door and looked outside just as the ax came down.

CRACK!

The tree limb split in two, the pieces tumbling to the ground. He placed another log on the block, straightened and wiped the sweat from his forehead. Despite the cool fall air, Ethan was wearing a thin T-shirt, jeans and boots. She cocked an eyebrow as he raised the ax again, his sweat-soaked shirt clinging to the bulging muscles in his back, and slammed the ax into the wood.

He yanked the ax out of the split, paused and straightened his back. Sensing her, he slowly looked over his shoulder and his eyes met hers instantly.

Jolene pushed out of the screen door as he set the ax down.

"Lose track of time?"

A confused expression crossed his face.

She walked across the small backyard to the pile of limbs. "You said to be here at eight."

He glanced at his watch. "And you are. Good job."

As she walked up to him, his gaze shifted to her bruised cheek, and his face dropped. "How's your eye?"

"It's fine." Before leaving her apartment, she'd done the best she could at concealing the black eye she'd received from being hit by his truck the night before. But apparently, concealer didn't do the trick.

He opened his mouth to say something and she raised her hand, shaking her head. "Nope. You already apologized and I accepted your apology. End of story. There's nothing else to say about it."

He stared at her for a moment. Finally, he nodded and said, "Alright."

She glanced down at his ax and irritably clicked her tongue. "Anyway, you told me to be here at eight, but you're obviously busy."

He looked down at the pile of firewood he'd spent the morning chopping. "How do you know I didn't call you here to help me chop wood?"

She put her hands on her hips and narrowed her eyes. "Let's get one thing straight, Ethan. I agreed to help you find Slade Packer. Nothing else."

He bent down and picked up a thick log. "That's right, and in return, I agreed *not* to turn you in to the FBI."

"You also promised that the FBI would wipe my slate clean after I help you find him."

"Take him down."

"That's what I said."

"No, you said find him."

She rolled her eyes. "Same thing."

He tossed her a small branch. "No, it's not. I could find Packer any day of the week. I need you to help me get evi- dence to *take him down*. Big difference."

"Yeah, I get it."

He handed her a block of wood. "Do you?"

"Do you understand that I could run in two seconds? Hell, I could've this morning. You'd never find me. I'd be on a beach somewhere sipping the world's finest tequila and you'd be right where you are now. No closer to *taking down* Packer."

He piled another piece of wood into her arms, raised his eyebrows, and pulled his cell phone from his pocket. As he dialed, he said, "How about if I just call Mike Woodson right now? Let him know where you are?"

She kicked the phone out of his hands and like a flash of lightning, he caught it mid-air and looked at her with steely eyes. "That's not how we treat our electronics."

She glared at him as he slid the phone back into his pocket.

"Grab that log."

As he turned and started walking toward the house, she said, "Or, what?"

He paused, and turned back. "Is this how it's going to

be? Because this little attitude of yours sure is starting to grind on my nerves."

"You haven't seen attitude yet." They stared at each other like two boxers about to fight. Finally, she took a deep breath. "I don't like being handled, Ethan. I'm not used to it." She looked down, the fight momentarily fleeing from her eyes. "You have me by the balls, Ethan —so to speak. And I don't like it."

He cocked an eyebrow. "Miss Reeves, if I had you by the balls, you'd know it." He held her gaze for a moment before turning and walking back to the cabin.

As if being dragged by a ball and chain, Jolene followed him into the cabin.

"So why am I here exactly?"

"Wood goes in the den; front room on your left."

She walked down the hall and he called out after her. "Want some coffee?"

She carelessly dumped the wood next to the fireplace and walked back into the kitchen. "Coffee sounds good, thanks."

"Alright." He scooped the grains into the coffee maker. "Sit at the table."

"Please."

"Please."

She sank into the chair. "Why am I here?"

"Well, last night you and I agreed to an arrangement. It starts today."

"At eight o'clock in the morning, huh?"

"The morning is the most productive part of the day."

"For you, apparently."

He leaned against the counter and crossed his arms

over his chest as the coffee brewed. "Are you not a morning person?"

"That's an understatement."

"As long as you're working with me, we'll get an early jump on the day."

She inhaled and shook her head. "You're liking this too much."

He grinned.

The coffee pot dinged and Ethan filled two cups to the rim. "So like I said, it starts today. This morning, we're going to make our plan." He walked over and handed her the cup. "Cream or sugar?"

"Both."

After retrieving the condiments from the cupboard, he slid into the seat across from her.

"My first question is—what exactly do you do, Miss Reeves?"

"Can't you check the FBI file you have on me?"

"Oh, I have. I just want to hear your side."

"Make sure I don't lie to you, huh?"

"Precisely."

She ripped open a sugar packet and stirred it into her coffee. "I'm a financial consultant."

He rolled his eyes. "A crooked financial consultant."

She stared at him for a moment. "Okay, we'll cut the bullshit. Yes, I hide assets."

"Tax evasion."

"You could call it that."

"Is that all you do?"

"Now? Yes."

"What did you do before this?"

"Cybertheft for a bit, and I… did some money laundering and transferred funds for clients. A money mule, as you would call it."

"Stolen funds."

"Correct."

"And why'd you get out of that?"

She sipped, contemplated her answer. "Conscience, I suppose."

"The cyber thief had a change of heart?"

"You could say that."

"Why?"

Her eyes cut him. "That's my business, Ethan."

He raised his eyebrows. "Alright, alright. So why did you make the jump to tax evasion?"

"I'm good at it."

"Who hires you?"

"Now? Corporations, mostly."

He shook his head and blew out a breath. "Corporations? Would I be shocked to know who?"

"Absolutely. Some Fortune 500 companies." She leaned back in her chair, nonchalantly. "Honestly, Ethan, I don't blame them for what they do. The government puts so many taxes and restrictions on American companies, it's only smart for them to hide and move money offshore. You never know what the future holds, and they're just covering their asses."

"You're covering their asses."

"I assist in it, yes."

"You do it."

"Yes. I have no tie to them whatsoever so it's untraceable. And I get paid nicely for it."

"And does this give you a clean conscience?"

"Absolutely, I sleep very well at night." She leaned forward, sipped. "What I'm doing might be illegal, Ethan, but I'm not hurting anyone. I'm not stealing from anyone. I'm just helping people manage their money."

"Women can justify anything."

She grinned. "We sure can. Does that match your FBI file on me?"

"Mostly… I'd love to know who you worked for in the cybertheft ring."

She shook her head. "Not part of the deal, Ethan. You know that. I was clear on that last night. I help you with Packer, you wipe my slate clean. That *does not* involve ratting out everyone that I've worked with in the past."

We'll see about that, he thought. "Okay, onto the task at hand. Are you familiar with the Hexagon Group?"

"Of course."

"What do you know about them?"

"Only hearsay, but they've got a solid reputation… for dodging the law at least."

"Do you work for them, Jolene?"

"No."

"Have you ever?"

"No."

"Have you ever met Packer?"

She shook her head. "No, but I've heard of him."

"In connection with the Hexagon Group?" She paused for a moment, and then said, "Yes."

"Is he a part of the group?"

"My assumption is, yes."

"The leader?"

"That I don't know." When Ethan cocked his head, she said, "Seriously, I don't know. No one seems to know a lot about him, but his name is associated with numerous government hacks. Impressive hacks—the most recent being on the Pentagon. No telling how many government secrets that guy has in his arsenal. The rumor is that he's got a small group of people working for him, developing malware and doing God knows what else." She sipped her coffee. "And he pays his staff well. Everyone in my... profession wants to work for him. But no one can seem to get to him, or in some cases, they're too scared to even try."

"What do you mean scared?"

"He punishes disloyalty."

"How?"

She laughed. "Man, for being employed by the FBI, you sure don't know much."

"Enlighten me."

"He kills them, Ethan. If someone goes behind his back, or hell, if he just suspects that they are, he kills them." She sipped. "Kind of surprised you don't know that."

"Do you have names?"

"Of the people he's killed?"

"Yeah."

"No. And even if I did, I don't have proof." Pause. "So what's your plan for getting to this guy?"

He grinned, and stood. "Follow me."

He led her down the hall, into the den, and motioned her to sit on the couch while he retrieved his laptop from the coffee table.

He sank into the cushion next to her and as the laptop powered up, he said, "Packer has so many layers of security built around him, it's unbelievable, but I happened to stumble upon a few things."

He began logging into multiple secured systems. "I scanned through the employee files that he hacked into at the Pentagon…"

Jolene cut in. "The employee files that he is *suspected* of hacking into. We don't know if it was him."

"Right. Anyway, what baffles me is that he had access to thousands of employees, so why only a short list of twenty? Why them? What the hell is the connection? So I cross-referenced the files and although I'm not sure what information he pulled, one common thread is wealth."

"Everyone is rich?"

"Everyone's definition of rich is relative, but, yes."

She cocked her head and looked at him. "What is your definition of rich?"

His fingers stopped tapping on the keyboard as he stared blankly at the screen.

She smirked, "Wow, it's not a trick question or anything."

He looked at her. "What's yours?"

Without hesitation, "Money."

"Of course it is, you criminal."

She nudged him in the ribs.

"Anyway, back to the subject, so the obvious assumption is extortion; blackmail."

"You mean he holds the personal information that he hacked as blackmail?"

"Right."

"Has anyone reported being blackmailed?"

He shook his head. "No, but that doesn't necessarily

mean that it didn't happen. Packer could have gained access to personal email accounts, banking accounts, medical records, whatever. He could expose affairs, illegal trading, selling secrets, anything."

"And whoever is being blackmailed would be more than happy to pay the ransom to save their butts."

"Exactly, and no one else would know about it."

"I see. So that's what you found? Doesn't sound like much to link to Packer."

"I'm not finished." He clicked a few more keys and an image popped up on his screen. "Recognize him?"

She leaned forward and peered at the black and white picture. "Nope."

"That's Bia Wu. He is one of the twenty who was hacked."

"Who is he?"

"He's a genius software engineer who worked for the Department of Defense until accepting a job with the NRC last year."

"NRC?"

"Nuclear Regulatory Commission."

She raised her eyebrows.

"Yeah, exactly. And he has a past."

"What kind of past?"

"Breaking and entering, stealing."

"No shit?"

"No shit." He slid her the side-eye. "I thought you might know him."

She rolled her eyes. "I don't know every criminal in the world, Ethan."

He grinned. "Anyway, the government recruited him after graduating college with a doctorate in computer science."

"I didn't think someone with a record could work for the government."

"When you're a genius like Bia, you can. And besides, he was just a kid when he got busted."

"Okay, so we've got a list of rich people and Bia. Where are you going with this?"

"Isn't it obvious?"

"No."

"Let me lay it out for you. Slade Packer has a nasty hobby of hacking. Bia is a genius software engineer, who not only has direct access to government files but now has direct access to the United States' nuclear weapons arsenal." He scratched his head. "Maybe Packer is recruiting Bia, or blackmailing him, to gain access to our nukes."

"That's quite a theory, Ethan. What about the other nineteen people that were hacked?"

He shrugged. "Not sure. Could just be a ruse to make us chase our tails. Maybe all Packer really wanted was Bia."

"Please tell me you have more proof... or, hell, any proof at all."

"Nope. Just my gut instinct."

"Based on that comment, I'm assuming you haven't told your little theory to your fellow FBI comrades."

"Right. I'd like to explore this angle a bit before talking to them."

She crossed her arms over her chest and leaned back. "And how are you going to explore this angle?"

He looked at her and narrowed his eyes. "The question is—how are *you* going to explore this angle?"

CHAPTER 12

"YOU WANT ME to penetrate Packer's inner circle?"
No, because that's too dangerous, he thought. "Just
find out who's in it. Concrete evidence of who's in it.
That's it. Just get me names and I'll handle the rest."

"Just names?"

"Just names."

She pushed off the couch and began pacing. "And just
to be clear, I do this and you don't turn me over to the FBI,
and you wipe my slate clean."

"That's right."

She stopped in front of the window and put her hands
on her hips. The morning sun streamed in through the windows, outlining her curvy body. He licked his lips.

"If you don't keep your word, Ethan…"

He stood and was inches from her face in two swift
steps. "I might be a lot of things, Jolene, but I'm not a liar."

She looked into his steely eyes, lingered a moment
before saying, "Okay. I'm in."

"Good. Let's make a plan."

She glanced past him, down the hall. "Breakfast first. I'm starving."

"Okay, let me stoke the fire first."

"I'll handle the fire, you cook."

"You got it."

Fifteen minutes later, he set a plate stacked with eggs, bacon and toast in front of her.

"It's not gourmet or anything."

"It's perfect, thanks." She scooped up a forkful of eggs. "So let's say that I am able to identify Packer's crew, then what?"

"Names go a long way. If I can link them all together, I'll have enough to open an official investigation on Packer. But focus on Bia; my gut tells me there's something there." He sipped his coffee.

She bit into her toast. "Okay, I think I can do this. How long do I have?"

He glanced at the clock.

"You're kidding." She shook her head. "These things take time. I can't just go around asking too many questions about Slade Packer without anyone noticing. I have a reputation to uphold, you know."

"Hey, a deal's a deal. Figure it out."

"You can be very unpleasant, you know that?"

"Not nearly as unpleasant as your attitude."

"What attitude?"

He laughed.

She scooped up the last bite of eggs, sipped her coffee and leaned back in the chair. Her gaze locked on his and he knew she was about to tell him something. Something new.

She sighed and said, "Well, since you and I are going to work together now, there's probably something I should tell you."

"This is about Chase Martinez, isn't it?"

Her back straightened. Yep, he was right.

"I'll find out anyway, Jolene. You might as well tell me."

"I knew him."

"You *knew* him?"

"Yes."

"From where?"

"Work."

"*Work*. Are you serious?"

She nodded.

"Wait…" he paused. "Were you doing a job with him the day he was killed?"

"No. We had actually squared off from an old job."

"When was the last time you spoke with him?"

"A few days ago."

"Just a few days ago?"

She nodded.

"You're kidding."

She shook her head.

"Where? You know that will be on camera somewhere, right?"

She laughed, "No way, we met at a hole-in-the-wall bar, Dave's Bar, outside of town. There's no way in hell they have cameras or would even remember my face."

"So you and Chase meet up, then a few days later he shows up at your apartment and is killed. There's no way this is a coincidence."

"That's what bothers me."

"Had he contacted you?"

"No."

"Did he know where you lived?"

"I really don't think so, Ethan. He didn't know my alias name that I use here either."

"And you have absolutely no idea why he came to Barb's B&B? It's not a coincidence, Jolene."

"I mean, the logical thought is that he came to find me, but I don't know how the hell he knew where to look."

"Why would he try to find you, anyway?"

She looked down. "We, uh, didn't leave on good terms."

"Explain."

"He stiffed me out of my money... so I took his. And... accidentally broke his wrist in the process."

"Shit, Jolene. Seriously?"

"Yeah."

"So this guy finds where you are and intends to get his money back, and gets brutally murdered in the process."

"Appears that way."

"You have to tell the cops."

Her head snapped up. "No. No, Ethan." She blew out a breath. "What the hell am I supposed to say? I'm a criminal, and by the way my name isn't Anna, and, oh, I was one of the last people to see Chase Martinez alive. Let me go ahead and put my wrists together so you can handcuff me and take me to jail."

He stared at her for a moment, understanding her predicament.

She looked out the window. "Just leave it alone, Ethan."

"They can't arrest you for just talking to him."

"There's just too many layers to this situation, Ethan,

you know that." She stood and took her plate to the sink. "I just wanted to give you a heads up, okay?" She glanced at the clock. "Anyway, I've got to get going."

"What? Got a few big appointments today?"

"Actually, smartass, I do."

"Where are we going?"

"*We* aren't going anywhere."

He met her at the sink, looked her up and down, then narrowed his eyes, and closed the inches between them. "You already ran on me once, Miss Reeves."

He noticed her chest begin to rise and fall faster. He was able to get to her. Good. That's exactly what he wanted.

She started to open her mouth and he said, "You can argue with me, you can fight about it, you can cry about it, but Jolene, I'm going with you whether you like it or not." He slid his phone from his pocket. "Or I can just call my buddy at headquarters right now and let him know where you are."

After a moment, she rolled her eyes. "God, you're annoying."

The corner of his lip curved.

She wiped her plate, put it in the cupboard, and as she turned to leave the room she said, "Well, you better pack your bags."

"Where are we going?" He called out after her.

From down the hall, she said, "New York. And we're traveling *my* way."

He raised his eyebrows and said, "Alrighty, then."

And as he walked out of the room, he didn't notice the recorder hidden behind the picture frame.

∽

The plane skidded onto the runway, shaking Ethan from his deep sleep.

Jolene grinned as he opened his eyes. "Good afternoon, sunshine."

He straightened and glanced at his watch—4:30. Inhaling, he glanced out the small window at the hustle and bustle on the tarmac.

"Hello everyone, welcome to New York City. Please enjoy your stay and it was a pleasure having you on board with us this afternoon."

He blinked a few times and turned to Jolene. "I can't believe I fell asleep."

"Me, either. I don't think my grandma even goes to bed this early."

"You know, this is supposed to be my vacation. You can sleep anytime you want on vacation."

"That's true, I guess."

Ethan turned on his phone and scrolled through the messages. He raised his eyebrows—Diner Debbie. He clicked it open.

Hey you. How about dinner tomorrow night? The best BBQ in the world, as promised. Let me know. XOXO, Deb.

He glanced up to see Jolene grinning.

"Hey, didn't your mama teach you not to read other people's messages?"

"Definitely not. Hot date?"

Unsure how to answer, he was saved by the ding of the *buckle seatbelt* sign turning off. He jumped up and retrieved

Jolene's carry-on luggage from the overhead, handed it to her, then pulled his own down.

"You pack light for a girl."

"Thanks, I think."

As the crowd began filtering into the aisle, Ethan motioned to her. "Ladies first."

"That's so antiquated." She grinned as she stepped in front of him.

He leaned forward, into her ear. Goosebumps slid over her skin as she felt the warmth of his breath. He said, "You must not know many gentlemen, Miss Reeves."

Her stomach tickled, and embarrassed at the rush of adrenaline he gave her; she cleared her throat and kept her eyes straight ahead. This was business, nothing else.

She felt him close behind as they filed out of the plane and into the busy airport.

"My appointment is at seven tonight. Think you'll be able to entertain yourself?"

"I'll entertain myself by accompanying you."

She halted, turned toward him. "No, Ethan."

He kept his pace and walked past her. "Yep."

She groaned as she caught up. "You don't even... *dammit* Ethan."

He smiled.

"You'd need a tux."

This time he halted and turned toward her. "A *tux*?" As in, a tuxedo?"

He hated dressing up, especially in suits. And a tux? Well, that was a whole other level. Something about it. Not just how uncomfortable it was, but it just wasn't him. He didn't feel like himself in a damn tux. He'd rather be in a T-shirt, tattered jeans, and boots any day.

"Yeah, a tux. Are you familiar with a tuxedo?"

He ignored the jab. "Okay, then. I guess I'll need to find somewhere…"

"Don't worry about it, I'll handle it."

"What do you mean you'll handle it?"

"Exactly what I said. I'll get your tux."

"You don't even know what size I wear."

Her eyebrows tipped up. "Please. I sized you up the moment I met you."

"Objects in the mirror appear smaller than they actually are." He grinned.

She laughed and slapped his arm. "Pervert."

"Okay, so where are we going?"

"The Senator's Ball."

His eyes rounded. "You're kidding."

"Nope."

"And how the hell did you get an invite to that?"

"That's confidential."

His mouth fell open. "Don't freakin' tell me… don't tell me you do *business* with some of them."

"Okay, I won't."

He shook his head. "Geez, Jolene, how many people could I arrest if I just had your rolodex."

She laughed as they stepped outside. "More than a few. And I'm meeting a friend after."

"A friend? Is this a boyfriend or a work associate?"

"What's the difference?" She smirked. "Just joking. It's a work associate."

"A work associate that's going to help you pin down Packer's crew?"

"Exactly."

"Perfect."

"Thanks for your approval. How are you going to entertain yourself?"

"Oh, I'm going with you."

She stopped on a dime and spun toward him. "Absolutely not, and that is *not* negotiable."

"Sounds like a boyfriend to me."

She rolled her eyes and started walking. "Like I said, so annoying."

"I thought you said I was a gentleman."

"I said antiquated. Big difference."

"Not where I'm from."

"Seriously, Ethan, the person I'm meeting with won't talk if you're there." She looked him up and down. "You have FBI written all over you."

"Do I?" He rubbed his chin. "I should've kept the beard."

"Beard?"

"Oh, yeah. I could have hidden your purse in there. Shaved it just a few weeks ago."

She held up her large, expensive, leather tote. "Wow. Impressive."

"Yes, it was." He rubbed his bare chin. "RIP." Pause. "Okay, so you can go to your clandestine meeting but that's it, we do everything else together."

"Thanks for the permission."

He winked and grabbed her arm. "Taxi's this way."

She almost stumbled as she glanced up at the sign. "Thanks."

She seemed distracted; thrown off her game. And for some reason, he had an idea that it was him.

The electric doors slid open and the sounds of yells, shouts and incessant honking vibrated through the cool air, perfumed by exhaust pipes. Ah, the city.

As she fumbled through her purse, Ethan stepped to the curb.

"Jolene, over here." He motioned over to a cab.

"That was fast."

He opened the door and slid in after her.

"Where to?" The driver asked.

"The Plaza Hotel."

"You got it."

Ethan cocked his head. "The Plaza? Seriously?"

"Hey, I told you that if you were going to tag along, we were going to travel my way."

"Yeah, but," he shook his head and looked at her. "Never mind."

Her gaze was fixed on the road ahead and he suddenly realized he had so many questions about her. Who was she, really? She'd been a criminal all of her adult life, and half of her childhood, yet, behind all that toughness, there was a softness. Somewhere. Hidden deep inside. And if he had to guess, she did everything she could to keep it under wraps. But he could see it. It was there, definitely.

She turned and looked at him. "What?"

He grinned and narrowed his eyes. "You're an interesting one, Miss Reeves."

She cocked an eyebrow. "Yeah?"

"Yeah." He looked out the window. "The Plaza. I didn't really take you for a Plaza kind of girl."

"I like nice things."

"A change from Chicago?"

"Have you ever been to the slums of Chicago, Ethan? Where the unemployment rate is sixty percent?"

"No."

"If you had, maybe you'd understand the desire for luxury once you've left."

"Fair enough." He glanced down at her designer handbag. "Pay must be good in your… profession."

She ignored the comment and taking her cue, he quit asking questions, sat back, and enjoyed the view of the city whizzing past the windshield. Finally, the cab pulled to a stop in front of the hotel.

"I'll have your tux sent to your room after we check-in."

He started to protest, but bit his tongue. "Okay, thanks."

They scaled the red steps that led up to the luxury hotel.

"I'll see you in an hour." She paused, looking him over. "And I don't think that stubble goes with a tux."

He frowned and rubbed his chin as she winked, turned and walked away.

CHAPTER 13

ETHAN TUGGED AT the bowtie that felt like a noose around his neck as he knocked on her hotel door.

"Damn tux."

A minute ticked by and he knocked again. Finally, the door opened.

His jaw dropped, his body momentarily paralyzed.

Say something, you idiot. But the fog in his brain prevented him from putting words together.

She stood in front of him, statuesque, in a strapless black velvet dress. Her hair was pulled into an elegant bun on the top of her head, exposing her neck and bare shoulders.

His lips parted as he looked at her skin. It was pale, smooth and looked as soft as silk. He had to fight the urge to bend down into her neck, kiss lightly, and then work his way down.

Her dark eye makeup accentuated her alluring, whiskey brown eyes. Her lips, a shiny pink. God, he wanted to kiss them. Lick them. Hell, he wanted those lips *on him*.

He'd never seen her like this. Sure, he knew she was beautiful but his image of her had been built around a black leather jacket and the Glock on her hip. He'd never seen her dressed up—and overtly feminine.

His pulse picked up. My God, she was stunning. She was the most beautiful women he'd ever seen in his life.

A small smile crossed her lips. "You alright?"

Dammit, Ethan, say something.

"Yeah, I'm good." He cleared his throat. "This damn tux."

She smiled. "You look nice."

"Thanks, you too."

"Thanks. Did I cover the bruise okay?"

He winced. Her black eye that *he* had caused. "I didn't even notice it, so, yes. I'm still sorry about that."

"I told you not to worry about it. It's almost gone."

"You look... stunning."

She smiled. "Thank you. Just let me get my purse."

He lingered in the doorway—because he feared he'd jump her if he saw her next to a bed—and watched her walk across the hotel room. He felt his pants begin to tighten as her hips swayed left and right with each step. Sweat began to dampen his skin. What the hell was wrong with him?

He needed a drink. A stiff drink. STAT.

He quickly wiped the sheen from his forehead. "I thought about grabbing a drink at the bar on the way out."

She grabbed her purse and glanced at the clock. "Make it quick."

Two shots of whiskey later, Ethan escorted Jolene up the steps into the fancy hotel that hosted the evening's Senator's Ball.

He had to fight a smile as they walked up the steps. He was proud. Proud to have Jolene on his arm. But the thing was, it wasn't just because of her beauty, it was because of who he knew she was. Deep down inside. The woman she tried so desperately to hide away.

Fresh flowers perfumed the air as they stepped into the hotel.

"This way, please." A man, in a tux, of course, led them down a long hall.

"Thank you."

Ethan raised his eyebrows as they walked into the room. The biggest chandeliers he'd ever seen hung from the ceiling, casting a golden glow over the room, which was meticulously sprinkled with dozens of tables decorated with white tablecloths, fresh flowers, and candles. The low melody of jazz music played from the band in the back and a large bar flanked the side of the room. Waiters and waitresses walked around with platters full of caviar, oysters and the finest cheeses.

The room oozed wealth. New York's finest stood in groups, small talking, ass-kissing and making million-dollar decisions. Every person in the room had an agenda.

He'd been to plenty of hoity-toity FBI events but nothing this extravagant.

Heads turned as Jolene stepped into the room.

He leaned in her ear. "Who exactly do you know in this room?"

"A few people."

"A few people, huh?"

She smiled, "Let's get a drink."

As they walked to the bar, he said, "So what's your plan here? Just to make an appearance?"

"This is just as much networking for me as any-thing else."

"Networking for criminals. Nice."

"You assume criminal networking happens during moonless nights in dark alleyways, right?"

The barman walked up. "Good evening, what can I get you two to drink?"

"Champagne, please."

"Whiskey on the rocks." He leaned against the bar. "You must have forgotten that I work for the FBI, sweet-heart. I'm the first one to understand that criminal activity doesn't just take place in dark alleys." He leaned forward. "Do you know how many senators are on our radar right now?" He looked around. "I see two already."

She sipped her high dollar champagne. "Well, maybe it's a working night for both of us, then."

"I think you're right." He winked. "I'm going to make the rounds. Meet you back here in a few."

"You got it."

❧

Jolene eased gracefully through the crowd, stopping to make small-talk with those she knew, and careful to avoid those she wasn't supposed to know.

Secrets. Everyone had them and the room was full of them.

Time ticked on and she found herself leaning against the back wall, contemplating her next move, when her eyes were drawn to a man in the corner.

The hair on her arm prickled.

Although his face was covered by shadows, there was no doubt he was watching her. And something about him made her want to get as far away from him as possible.

"Who is he?"

Startled, she whipped around. "Ethan, geez, you scared me."

His expression intense, he repeated, "Who is he?"

"I don't know."

"He's been watching you all night."

"He has?"

"Yes."

Apparently, Ethan had been, too. She gazed back at the man.

"Let's go meet him, shall we?" He grabbed her arm.

"No, Ethan, come on. It could be anybody."

He pulled her through the crowd and as they drew closer to the mystery man, he turned, his face briefly illuminated by the light, then briskly walked out of the room.

Jolene grabbed Ethan's arm. "Stop. I know him."

"Who is he?"

"I did business with him a long time ago." Her eyes narrowed. "He's an asshole."

Ethan stared at her for a moment. "What did he do?"

"Nothing."

"Jolene, what did he do?"

Silence.

"He hit on you, didn't he?"

She took a deep breath. "Yes, and he didn't take no very kindly."

Ethan's head snapped toward the door. "Did he hurt you?"

"No, no, not at all. He was just an asshole." She grabbed

his face and turned it toward her. "Ethan, stop. It's no big deal. Calm down."

She could see by his flushed cheeks that he was not calming down, at all. So she grabbed his hand. "I think we're done here anyway. I've made my appearance; let's go."

He took one last glance toward the door where the man had exited, clenched his jaw, and the finally nodded. "Alright."

"Good, and I've got to go meet my friend; you head back to the hotel."

He frowned, obviously not liking the arrangement.

"Ethan, we've already been through this. You can't come."

He inhaled deeply. "You better text me as soon as you get back to the hotel."

"Of course."

∾

Jolene walked down the narrow alleyway and opened the door to Aces. The smell of stale cigarette smoke singed her nose as she stepped into the small, dark bar and paused at the entry way. She scanned the thin crowd— two men, solo, mid-fifties seated belly up to the bar and a young couple at the front table by the window.

She pulled off her gloves and walked to the bar.

"What can I get for you?" The heavily tattooed barman wiped his hands on his apron.

"Is Dylan here?"

He nodded over to the back corner which was shaded by darkness.

"Thanks."

Jolene walked over to the table and tossed her purse in the chair. "Nice theatrics."

Dylan smiled, "I've always preferred the darkness, you know that."

Dylan leaned forward, her porcelain skin against her jet-black hair almost glowed in the dim light. Although it had only been a few months since Jolene had seen her, she'd aged. She looked run down and tired.

Jolene slid into the seat across from her.

Dylan raised her eyebrows. "Dang, what are you so dressed up for?"

"Had a thing."

"Sounds fun. Drink?"

"No, thanks."

Dylan sipped her tequila. "How was your flight?"

"Uneventful, exactly the way I like it."

"Good. How's Arkansas?"

"It's nice. Beautiful."

"Not better than this city though."

Jolene surprised herself when she hesitated.

Dylan laughed. "You got a boyfriend down there?"

"No. Just work."

"Alright, keep your secrets. You were always good at that."

Jolene smiled. "Tell me about the job with Beckett Industries."

Dylan leaned back. "Do you know how big this job is, Jolene? You do this and your career is set. You'd never need to take another job if you didn't want to." She sipped her drink. "Hell, I'd do it if I had your skill set. I considered it."

"Yeah, about that. Since when did you double your fee?"

"Since I found you this job."

Jolene leaned back, narrowed her eyes. "That's a pretty big cut of my earnings."

"It's a pretty big job. But I negotiated with you, didn't I?"

Jolene crossed her arms over her chest. "You mentioned you had other people willing to do it if I said no. Who?"

"That's my business."

"You don't have anyone else, Dylan. You know it, and I know it."

Dylan narrowed her eyes.

"And because of that, and because you lied to me, you get five percent."

"Ten was the deal, after I came down from twenty."

"Can I get you something to drink?" The barman set a water down in front of Jolene.

"No thanks." Jolene sipped and paused while he walked away. A solid minute of silence ticked by. "Okay, ten percent but I need you to do something for me."

Dylan's hard expression melted into a laugh. "How did this turn around on me so quickly?"

Jolene winked. "You trained me well."

"Alright, what do you want?"

"I need you to look into something for me."

"Okay…"

"Have you heard of Slade Packer?"

Dylan's eyes widened. "Yeah, I know Packer… are you wanting to get involved with that?"

"Have you met him?"

She shook her head. "No one has."

"Surely someone has."

"Not that I know of. He's got a small, close-knit crew that works for him, and talks for him. I'm not even sure if they've met him. What do you want with him?"

"Who's in his crew? Who works for him?"

"I've heard rumors."

"I need a solid list."

"A list of Packer's crew? Hell, need anything else while I'm at it?"

"Can you do it?"

"I've… I've probably got someone I can talk to."

"I need the names ASAP."

Dylan sighed. "Of course you do."

"Also, a man named Bia Wu. He's potentially working with Packer, too. I need you to confirm that, and get me anything you can on him."

"Bia Wu? Never heard of him."

"Not surprised. He works for the Nuclear Regulatory Commission."

Dylan raised her eyebrows. "Jesus, Jolene, what have you gotten yourself into?"

"Nothing, as soon as you get me the info."

"Okay, I'll do my best."

Jolene raised her water glass. "Thanks. Cheers."

"I'd be happier with twenty percent."

Jolene laughed as Dylan pulled out an envelope from her purse and slid it across the table.

"This is all the information on Beckett Industries and the job. Read through it tonight and let me know what you think. The deal goes down next week, I believe."

Jolene slid the envelope into her purse and stood. "Thanks."

"My pleasure."

"Have a good night."

"You, too."

Jolene pushed out of the front door and inhaled the fresh air. She was never a fan of Aces, but it was Dylan's meeting place for all things business. So she had gotten used to it.

The night was dark and unusually quiet. Other than a few dumpsters and bags of trash, the narrow alleyway was vacant.

She looked from left to right, surprised to see no one at all. She gripped her purse straps, took a few steps and froze. A chill ran up her spine.

A shadowed figure emerged from behind the dumpster.

Her pulse spiked as she turned in the other direction, and another figure emerged behind her.

Here we go.

She widened her stance, every muscle in her body ready to react to what came next. Her heart raced as both men began closing in on her.

She had no gun, no knife, and no weapon.

Click.

The light reflected off a switchblade knife as the man in front raised his hand.

Adrenaline pumped through her veins as she balled her fist.

She spun around as the man behind her leapt forward and caught her wrist. She landed a right hook just as the other attacker grabbed her purse.

She hooked her arm around the strap and swung with her other arm, slamming it into the man's nose.

"You *bitch*!"

"Get her!"

As both men grabbed her, she heard steps pounding down the alley.

WHACK!

Blood spattered on her face, and she was released, her body tumbling to the ground.

"What the *fuck*?" She heard one man say just before he was punched in the jaw. His body locked, and slammed face first into the hard concrete. The other man leapt forward, knife in hand.

She scrambled to her feet, turned, and saw Ethan lunge toward her attacker.

The two men wrestled to the ground, legs kicking, fists flying.

Jolene jumped on the man's back as Ethan slid out from under him. Before she could register what was happening, the silver blade of a knife cut through the air inches from her face. She stumbled backward as the man lunged forward and raised his arm just above her head.

Her heart stopped as the knife came down.

Like a flash of lightning, Ethan caught the man's arm and bent it back. The bone snapped, followed by a bellow of agony.

He grabbed her arm and led her down the alleyway and onto the street.

"You okay?" He gripped her hand as they briskly walked down the sidewalk.

Chest heaving, she glanced over her shoulder. "Yeah…

yeah, I think so." She looked at him. His muscular chest rose and fell with adrenaline, his jaw was clenched, his eyes fierce. He looked nothing like the man she knew. This man was a fighter; a take-no-prisoners kind of fighter.

She wiped her face with the back of her hand. Blood. Not hers—someone else's.

"That was the guy, wasn't it? The guy that was watching you earlier?" He gripped her harder.

"Yes, I think so." Pain shot through her hand. "Ethan, Ethan you're hurting me."

He loosened his grip. "Sorry."

She looked over her shoulder again. "I don't see them."

"No, I don't imagine we'll see them again."

She blew out a breath. "Like I said, he was an asshole."

He grit his teeth. "You need to choose a different profession, Jolene."

Still wide-eyed, she stared at him for a few steps. "How did you know where I was?"

He led her around the corner to the hotel.

"Lucky guess."

"You followed me."

His expression didn't change as they walked into the hotel and stepped onto the elevator.

She looked up at him. "You don't trust me."

The door dinged, and still holding her hand, he led her out of the elevator, to her door. He paused and looked down at her, his face charged with intensity. She gazed back at him and he took a step forward, inches from her face.

Her heart fluttered, her pulse picked up. The electricity was thick between them.

In barely a whisper, she said, "Thank you."

His body towered over hers and for the first time in a long time, she felt small, vulnerable and in desperate need of a man's touch. His touch. Ethan's touch.

He slowly leaned down, his lips inches from hers.

His steely eyes narrowed and locked on hers. "Don't leave the hotel again."

CHAPTER 14

"MORNIN' BOYS. SIT where you'd like."

Jameson, Dean and Jonas slid into the corner booth in the back of the diner, which allowed for more privacy.

Donny's Diner was the proud hub of all things Berry Springs. Located in the middle of the square, the diner served a constant rotation of locals who came in not only for the fresh coffee and greasy Southern food, but also to get a dose of daily gossip. With its blue and white checkered curtains, bright red booths, American flags and old jukebox, time seemed to stand still in Donny's Diner.

"Well… if it ain't Berry Springs' finest. Mornin' officers."

"Howdy, Mrs. Booth."

With her signature bun on top of her head—always held together by a yellow number two pencil—Mrs. Booth was a staple at Donny's Diner. Born and raised in Berry Springs, Mrs. Booth was a tough-talking country gal and a favorite among the locals. She remembered every guest by name and every piece of gossip that came through her diner.

She slid three mugs onto the table and filled them with coffee. "How's it goin'?"

"Busy."

She leaned in, her eyes widened. "I'll bet it is. Anything new with that murder over at Barb's?"

"Not that we can discuss, Mrs. Booth."

"Oh, come on, Jameson. You know I won't tell a soul. I heard he was from out of town. Florida, right?"

Jameson glanced around the table. No matter how many times the department was warned against spreading confidential information, it still happened with every case. *Every damn case.*

"What was he doing in Berry Springs? Do we know?" *We.*

"We're working on it, Mrs. Booth."

"Alright, fine, keep your secrets. Um... what about those bones found out at Otter Lake?"

"We're working on that, too."

She took a shaky, deep breath. "I hope y'all figure it all out, soon. Gives me the damn chills." She straightened her back. "Anyway, what can I git for y'all?"

Jameson leaned back and rubbed his stomach. "Just coffee and a Super Slam for me, please ma'am."

"Pancakes, bacon, ham, cheese grits and toast. You got it, Jameson. And, you boys?"

Jonas clicked his phone off. "French toast, thanks."

"Alrighty. Dean?"

"Pancakes. Double-stack."

She scribbled on her notepad and said, "Be out shortly."

Jameson took a sip of coffee. "We got the BPA results back on the B&B murder. Came in late last night."

Dean leaned forward. "Well?"

"First, I should tell you that it was confirmed that the blood in the tub, and on the walls, is Chase's."

Jonas rolled his eyes. "I could've told you that."

"And there were no traces of anyone else's."

"Dammit. Not Mark Williams or his girlfriend?"

"Right."

"Son of a bitch."

"Yep. The BPA analyzed the shape and tails of the blood spatters, on the walls specifically, and get this, the patterns suggest a blunt force of some kind had to have occurred."

Dean frowned. "But he was stabbed to death."

"That's what it looked like when I saw him. But that's not the story the blood spatters tell."

"Jameson, that kid was stabbed a dozen times, no doubt about it. I know what stab wounds look like, and that's what was done to him. We looked him over before turning him over to the medical examiner—there was no blunt hit anywhere on his body. Not one that would have sprayed that much blood, at least."

"Hey, I'm not saying I don't agree. I'm just letting you know that the official BPA report says—the way the blood hit the wall suggests blunt force, not stabbing."

"Something doesn't add up."

"Agreed." Jameson glanced at Jonas. "Do we have the official autopsy back, yet?"

"Not as of six this morning—an hour ago."

"Keep checking. That will tell us more, but as of right now, that's what we know."

In deep thought, Dean absentmindedly began rolling his napkin between his fingers. "One thing's for sure, stab wounds wouldn't spray on the wall like that." Pause. "It is *definitely* Chase's blood on that wall?"

"Yep."

Jonas spun his phone on the table. "What if the knife severed an artery?"

Dean sipped his coffee. "Yeah, that could cause blood to spray but not in this case. Chase Martinez wasn't stabbed in the neck, or through any major arteries."

"So then, how the hell did his blood get on the wall?"

Jameson raised his eyebrows. "Well, to confuse this even more, there was more in the report…"

"Here you go boys." Mrs. Booth slid three steaming plates across the table and added a basket of warm biscuits, with butter and strawberry jelly.

"Thanks Mrs. Booth." Jameson continued, "The angle which the blood hit the wall was a swift, upward facing, curved motion."

"Keep going…"

"When you compare that information with location of the open wounds on his body… he would have had to been doing some impressive aerobics to make those spatters."

Dean scratched his head while Jameson dug into his eggs as if they weren't speaking about a murdered man.

"So in other words, there's absolutely no way his wounds could have made those spatters. Even though it's his blood."

Feverishly chewing, Jameson nodded and said, "Yep. Riddle me that."

Dean blew out a breath and dug into his pancakes. A few minutes of silence ticked by, and suddenly, his eyes lit up. "What a second."

Jameson and Jonas both looked up from their plates.

"Someone put Chase's blood on the wall."

Jonas cocked his head. "What?"

A second slid by before Jameson's mouth fell open. "Holy shit."

Jonas shook his head, confused. "Wait. Why the hell would someone spray his blood on the wall? And then leave his stabbed body in the bathtub? I mean, why go to the effort to get his blood on the walls? He was obviously stabbed to death, so what difference does having his blood on the walls make?"

Dean grinned. "Because Chase wasn't killed in the bathroom, and the murderer is trying to set Mark and Tiffany up. It's a setup."

With a mouth full of ham and eggs, Jameson raised his eyebrows and said, "Holy shit, you could be right." He winked. "You'd make a hell of a detective, Dean."

Dean leaned back. "It makes sense, right? Hell, it's the only thing that makes sense."

Still chewing on this new theory, Jonas said, "If Chase wasn't killed in the bathroom, then where? And why the hell is someone framing Mark and Tiffany? I mean, why them?"

They sat in silence for a moment, baffled.

"Chase wasn't killed long before we got there and the amount of blood in the bathtub makes me think he had to have been killed close by, because otherwise, that much blood wouldn't have drained in the tub... it would have drained wherever he was killed."

"So that's what we need to investigate. Where Chase was really killed."

Jameson rubbed the scruff on his chin. "But we didn't find any more blood in the house... if Chase was killed somewhere other than Barb's B&B, how the hell did the murderer keep the trail clean?"

Stumped, Dean looked at Jameson, who looked at Jonas, who was gazing at Diner Debbie's chest.

Dean kicked him under the table as Jameson said, "She's nice to look at, Jonas, but we've got a murder we're trying to solve."

"Sorry."

"And besides, didn't you say you were gonna ask out Anna Gable?"

"Ah, Anna Gable." He put his hand over his heart. "I plan on it, next time I see her."

"Speaking of which, what did we dig up on her?" Dean glanced around the table at the blank stares. "Okay... no one's looked into her yet."

"Guess not."

Jonas sat up. "I'm on her. I mean, *it*. Dammit." His cheeks flushed. "I'm on *it*."

Jameson laughed and shook his head.

"Don't worry; I know how to keep it in my pants, unlike you, my friend."

Smirking, Jameson said, "It's hard to keep anything this big contained." He sipped his coffee and signaled for the check. "Alright guys, let's get to the station, and later we'll do another walk-through of Barb's B&B."

⁓

Nerve's fluttered in Jolene's stomach as she walked up the steps to the B&B and nodded at the officer. What the hell were they doing back?

She'd just gotten off the red-eye from New York, and the last thing she needed right now was another interview. Or another chance for them to figure out that her real name was not Anna Gable.

"Good afternoon, ma'am."

"Good afternoon." She pushed through the front door and glanced up the staircase, where the second floor was illuminated with fluorescent lights. She turned toward the muffled voices coming from the kitchen and after a moment, set down her luggage and walked down the hall.

"Anna, welcome back." Barb looked up from the kitchen table, her face pale with exhaustion, her eyes shaded with dark circles. Greg sat across from her.

"Hi, Barb; hey, Greg. What are the police doing back?"

"Doing another walk-through, I guess."

"They seemed pretty damn thorough the first time."

"Now they want to search the whole house."

Jolene glanced down the hall. "Have they arrested anyone yet?"

"Not that I know of. Such a damn mess, not to mention hell for my business."

Jolene glanced at Greg. "How are you? I thought Barb gave you a few days off?"

"Doing alright. I came by to check on her."

Barb nodded, her fingers spinning her coffee mug in a slow circle on the table. "Greg's been by to check on me every day, sweet thing." She sipped her coffee started to stand. "I'm sorry, dear, I forgot my manners. Do you want some coffee, Anna?"

"That sounds fantastic, but I can get it."

"I'll get it." Greg jumped up. "You sit."

"Thanks."

Barb sank back in her chair. "Detective Jameson's down at the dock now. I don't know what the hell he's looking for down there."

"Maybe the murderer came by boat."

"I guess that's plausible."

Greg grabbed a cup from the cupboard. "Or maybe he's looking for more bones."

Barb blew out a breath. "A murder at my house, and human bones found in Otter Lake. What's next? God, I hope he doesn't find any more bones. Especially here."

"Or hope that he does. The more bones they find, the better chance they have of a positive I.D., and understanding of what happened to him... or her."

"I guess you're right. The sooner they get an I.D. the sooner all this crap goes away."

"Do you think the bones are related? To the murder here?"

"No way. I mean, how? Why? Regardless, I want them to solve the murder *first*, bones second."

Greg handed Jolene her coffee and sat down. "I overheard the cops talking outside earlier. They said that the guy's name was Chase Martinez."

Jolene's stomach plummeted.

Barb nodded. "From somewhere out of town. Have you ever heard the name?"

She hesitated, looked down. "Don't think so."

"Me either."

"What about the guests who were staying in the room? Mark and Tiffany, was it?"

"Yes, Mark Williams and Tiffany Lancaster. The cops questioned them for hours but couldn't link them to Chase. They're back in their hometown I guess."

Greg wrinkled his nose. "Couldn't link them? But the guy was murdered in their room. They've got to be overlooking something."

Exhaling, Barb said, "Well, whatever the hell it is, I hope they find it fast and arrest whoever did this. I want things to get back to normal."

A moment of silence slid by, and the image of Chase's pale, stabbed body lying in the bathtub popped into Jolene's head. She shivered. She'd never seen a dead body before and she sure hoped that one would be her last.

Greg laughed, "You never know, Barb, business might pick up. There are a lot of sickos that will probably want to stay in the same room where someone was murdered. Look what it did for the Half Moon Hotel."

Built in the 1800s, The Half Moon Hotel was rumored to be haunted. People from all over the world came to visit the old hotel and would request to stay in one of the many haunted rooms. It was busy, year-round.

"That's true, I guess." Barb sighed. "Enough talk about death." She turned to Jolene. "How was your trip?"

"Good. Quick."

Greg leaned forward. "Where did you go?"

"New York."

"What for?"

"Work."

Barb smiled. "I do love New York. It's such a lovely city. Romantic."

Greg squeezed his face. "Romance. Who needs it?"

Barb smiled. "Greg, everyone needs romance. Everyone needs love. Life is…" she waved her hand in the air, "Life is bleak without it. Dark."

Greg looked down, uncomfortable all of a sudden.

"I've told you a million times now, Greg, you need to find you a good woman and settle down."

His eyes remained fixed on his coffee and Jolene swore she saw his cheeks flush.

Barb looked at Jolene, "And same goes for you, young lady. So tell me more about this Ethan boy."

"He's just a boy. That's it." She smiled.

"Just a friend?"

She hesitated. "Just a friend."

"A friend who comes by late at night?"

Jolene slid Barb the side-eye. "Yes."

Barb laughed. "What does this Ethan do?"

"He's… in computer forensics."

She raised her eyebrows. "Sounds exciting."

"About as exciting as this conversation."

Barb laughed boisterously. "Alright, alright, I won't pester you anymore. Just don't be single all your life, okay?"

Jolene smiled. "There's nothing wrong with being single."

Greg's head shot up. "Damn straight." He cocked his

head and looked at Barb. "What about you, Barb? Where's your love interest?"

"Oh, honey, he died twenty years ago."

"None since then?"

"Nope."

"I'm sorry."

"Oh, no, don't be. That's life. People come and go and the world keeps spinning."

"Why haven't you found anyone else?"

Barb sipped and shrugged. "I have other things to occupy my time now."

"Ms. Barb, we're all done here." Dean's towering body stepped into the room, his eyes scanning from Greg to Jolene.

"Thank God. No offense."

He smiled. "Sorry, that should be the last time."

She nodded and pushed out of her chair. "I want to catch the son of a bitch as much as you do."

"I know, and we will." Dean took another glance at Jolene, his gaze lingering a moment too long. And then, he looked around the table. "Have a nice day."

"Bye, Dean."

CHAPTER 15

ETHAN STEPPED OUT of the shower, his back stiff from the three-and-a-half hour plane ride back to Berry Springs. He dried off, walked to the bedroom, flicked on the TV and turned up the local evening news.

"... *still investigating a homicide at a local bed and break-fast. No word yet on the identity of the victim, or if they have a suspect, or a motive. As always, we'll keep you updated on this developing story. In another top story, we are still awaiting the DNA results to confirm the identity of the body found in Otter Lake earlier this week. Early estimates are that the bones are at least a few years old...*"

He paused, his gut clenching. What was it about the bones that didn't sit well with him? Why did he feel there was more to the story than meets the eye? And why did his gut tell him that maybe his decision to vacation in Berry Springs was... destiny?

He shook the thought out of his head and walked over to his suitcase. He rummaged through the clothes and pulled out a T-shirt and jeans, but hesitated. Maybe he should wear a collared shirt? He was going on a *date*, right?

If it were a date, why the hell was he dreading it so much?

He yanked out a blue-collared shirt, sniffed it to confirm its cleanliness, and slid it on. Next, jeans and boots.

He glanced in the mirror, ran his fingers through his wet hair and after a quick debate, dabbed on some cologne.

He took one quick glance at his work email, then grabbed his keys and jumped into his truck. As he started the engine, he glanced up at the sky. Almost a full moon. Usually, he thought a full moon was beautiful, but tonight, there was something... creepy to it.

He turned on the radio, bumped down the steep driveway and turned right onto County Road 3228.

His fingers bounced to the beat of classic rock as he turned onto the highway. Immediately, a pair of headlights cut through the darkness behind him.

The vehicle seemed to come out of nowhere.

He squinted, peering into the rearview mirror. An old, red single-cab truck—just like the one that pulled into his driveway a few evenings ago.

He slowed down, and so did the truck.

He sped up, and so did the truck.

Alright, he could play this game.

The truck stayed on his tail as he skillfully navigated the narrow, curvy mountain roads. As they rolled into town, he slowed and turned left onto the first residential street he came to, and slowed down. Moments later, the truck turned onto the same street. He maneuvered back onto the highway, slowed, and gazed into the rearview mirror.

The red truck emerged from the side street.

Yep, he was definitely being followed. What the hell? He

needed to get the license plate, which meant that he somehow needed to get behind the truck.

He scanned the streets ahead, his sights landing on a grocery store. Perfect.

He flicked on his turn signal, allowing the truck behind him to see where he was going, turned into the lot, and slipped into a tight spot between two big-rigs.

Seconds later the truck pulled in, but stopped suddenly at the entrance. Ethan watched as a moment passed, then the truck reversed, and pulled back onto the highway.

Dammit.

He slammed into reverse and pulled out onto the highway.

No sight of the red truck.

Damn, damn, damn.

He glanced at the clock—already five minutes late for his date with Debbie. Shit. He flicked on his turn signal and kept his head on a swivel as he drove to the square.

Who the hell would be following him? And more importantly, why?

"So how are you liking Arkansas so far?"

Jolted out of his haze of boredom, Ethan's gaze shifted from the deer-faced wall clock with antlers shooting out of its sides, back to Debbie across the table. Dammit, how long had he been zoned out?

"It's definitely different than DC, but I like it. It's a nice change of pace, and it's beautiful here." Desperate to do anything to ease the awkwardness, he picked up his fork and poked around at the mashed potatoes he'd barely touched.

She laughed. "I bet it is. Probably super boring to you… nothing exciting ever happens around these parts."

He looked down and immediately thought of Jolene— beautiful Jolene. Boring? No. Exciting? Hell, yes. Even if she did have a heck of an attitude on occasion. But over the last few days, he'd realized that little attitude of hers was part of her charm. Her attitude was a reflection of the strong woman she had become. Guarded, but strong.

He clenched his jaw. Here he was, sitting across from one of the sexiest women in town, and all he could think about was Jolene.

Laughter rang out from the pool tables in the back and hoping for entertainment of any sort whatsoever, he glanced over. Four burly, bearded men in T-shirts, Wranglers and cowboy hats exchanged handfuls of cash, presumably betting on their game.

He squinted and leaned forward, zeroing in on one of the men. Was that guy's lip really that big, or was it just the largest wad of tobacco he'd ever seen? He watched him grab a white Styrofoam cup from the table. Yep, it was tobacco. He then looked at the other two men hovering around the pool table. Were they dipping, too? Does everyone around here dip? What does dip even taste like?

"So, um, I bet you're used to all sorts of excitement with your job, huh?"

Dammit, he'd zoned out again.

Focus, Ethan.

He smiled. It was comical how every woman on the planet drooled when the words 'I work for the FBI' were muttered. Little did Debbie know, Ethan's job was spent working seventy-hour work weeks, sitting behind a grey, colorless desk decorated with computer screens. Not running shirtless through a sea of bullets with a busty damsel in distress over his shoulder.

Her eyelashes fluttered and she leaned forward. "You're in cyber… stuff, right?"

He smiled. "Yes, cybercrimes. I'm a computer forensics investigator."

"Sounds so cool. So what do you do exactly?"

He shifted in his seat. "I get assigned to cases involv- ing some sort of cybercrime and I look for evidence to help solve the case."

"Like, hacking and stuff?"

"Mostly, yeah."

"Cool." She grinned and narrowed her eyes. "Can you tell me about the case you're working on now?"

"I'm technically not working right now."

"Right. Vacation. But, I mean, you know, before you left."

He shook his head. "I'm pretty sure that could get me fired."

She wrinkled her nose and leaned back.

A moment slid by before her eyes widened and she leaned forward. "Wait. Does it have to do with that girl that was pulled from the lake a few days ago? Is that why you're really here?"

"Hate to disappoint you, but I really am here on vaca- tion." He paused. "You said 'girl.' Have they identified the bones already?"

"Oh, I don't know for sure, that's just the gossip—that it's a girl, I mean, female. I heard that they think her body was down there more than a year. *Years*. Can you imagine? Some- one dumped her body years ago and her poor family had no idea what happened, or where she's been." She paused. "I bet you deal with that kind of stuff a lot, huh?"

Missing persons didn't fall under his department, for the most part, but he didn't feel like going into all that.

"Sometimes, I guess."

"Oh."

A solid minute of silence slowly ticked by.

"Um, would you like another beer?"

As much as I would like an enema, he thought but didn't say it.

Debbie really was a nice girl and sure nice to look at. She had that Southern cowgirl thing going for her, like most girls did in Berry Springs, but unfortunately, there was zero chemistry between them and what had started out as a friendly dinner over barbecue had turned into a painstakingly awkward date.

This is exactly why he avoided dates, and women for that matter. Too much pressure. He didn't need a circus and fireworks on a first date, no, but he hoped for an occasional laugh, maybe an intriguing conversation, and a solid attraction.

Just like he had with Jolene.

And Debbie sure as hell was no Jolene.

He straightened his back and forced a smile.

"No more beer. I'm good, thanks."

She shifted in her seat, her big brown eyes darting across the table, unsure where to take the conversation next. "Coffee, then?"

Oh, man, she wasn't giving up. It was time to implement an exit plan. STAT.

He cleared his throat. "No thanks. Actually, I'm beat… I think I'm going to head back to the cabin."

He watched her shoulders slump as she looked down at

the table. He almost began to feel bad, but he had no doubt some cowboy would snag Debbie up soon enough and she'd forget about the disastrous first date with Ethan Veech.

He signaled for the check, and within minutes they stepped out the front doors and onto the sidewalk.

Grateful to be outside, he inhaled the cool, evening air, scented with the spice of the fall. He glanced around the gravel parking lot, looking for her car. It might have been a disastrous date but he was going to be a gentleman and walk her to her car.

"Where's your car?"

"Oh, I parked on the square and walked down. I thought I'd swing by the diner on my way home."

"Okay, I'll walk you."

"No, that's okay." Apparently, he wasn't the only one desperate to end the cringe-worthy date.

"Are you sure?"

"Yeah."

"Okay, um, well, it was good to see you, and you were right, it was the best barbecue in the world." Lie.

Awkward pause.

"Alright, well, have a good evening, Ethan."

"You, too."

Another awkward pause before engaging in the most awkward hug ever.

Ethan watched her walk down the sidewalk before turning and heading for his car. He glanced at his watch. Nine o'clock.

What to do now, he wondered, and his thoughts immediately went to one place.

CHAPTER 16

DING.

Jolene muted the television.

Ding.

Who the hell would be visiting her now? She pushed off the couch and padded over to the intercom. "Hello?"

"Hey, it's Ethan. You busy?"

She raised her eyebrows and glanced at the clock—9:30.

"No, I'll be down in a minute to let you in."

Butterflies fluttered in her stomach as she jogged down the staircase and peered through the peephole. She smoothed her hair and opened the door.

He smiled. "Hi."

"Hi."

"Your black eye's gone."

"Good as new."

He shifted his weight. "I was in town for dinner and just wanted to swing by and see if you'd learned anything about Packer."

So that's why he'd dropped by. She shook her head. "Not yet."

He raised his eyebrows. "Clock's ticking, Reeves."

"I've kinda had a lot going on the last few days, Veech."

"Like finding a dead body in the bathroom."

"That, and dealing with a certain annoying FBI agent."

He grinned.

A breeze blew in and she caught a scent of his cologne. A clean, fresh scent. Not too much. And definitely sexy. Her thoughts clouded.

They lingered in the doorway for a moment.

She held the door open and stepped back. "Come in."

He stepped over the threshold and looked around the dark house. "Still no guests?"

"No, Barb wants to wait until everything calms down a bit before putting the vacancy sign back up."

"Understandable." He followed her up the dark, wooden staircase and she could feel his eyes on her. "Any developments that you know of?"

She hesitated. "Not that I've heard."

They reached the second floor and he paused.

"Mind if I take a look?"

She halted, turned. "You want to see the bathroom?"

He nodded.

She wrinkled her nose in disgust. "Why?"

"Blame it on my occupation."

"You just want to look at it?"

"Yep."

"Are you not telling me something, Ethan?"

He stepped next to her. "Why so suspicious?"

"Blame it on my occupation."

He grinned. "Touché."

"Well, are you?"

"You mean, am I not."

She rolled her eyes. "Come on Ethan. Is the FBI taking the case or something?"

"Why would they?"

"I don't know, but if they are, I'd say I need to get the hell out of here, fast. So I'd appreciate the heads up."

He stared at her for a moment before saying, "I told you I'd take care of you."

The words were like a comforting blanket to her. She hadn't realized how much she'd needed to hear that.

He continued, "No. The FBI isn't taking the case. No reason to. Looks like a single, cut and dry murder in little ol' Berry Springs. Nothing to bring in the federal government for." He crossed his arms over his chest. "Unless *you* know something that I don't."

She laughed a humorless laugh. "You know, this little partnership of ours isn't going to work if neither of us trusts the other. Come on, you sicko, I'll let you see the bathroom."

She stepped over the yellow tape, and he followed. "Don't touch anything."

He shot her a *duh* look before walking into the bedroom.

He stopped and looked around.

"No point in looking around, really, they've turned everything upside down, bagged it up and sent it off."

He'd been to plenty of crime scenes where small-town law enforcement left a treasure trove of evidence undiscovered. Not that it was their fault really; it was just that their eyes weren't trained like an FBI employee.

He crossed the room and glanced out the window.

She motioned to the bathroom. "Here. You want to hurry this up? I'm not exactly loving being in this room again."

"Blood make you queasy?"

"Dead bodies make me queasy."

He stopped, his eyes inquisitive. "Have you seen a dead body before?"

"Believe it, or not, no."

He nodded, his eyes softened. "Time will help fade the image, I promise. But the memory will always be there, and you'll learn to live with it."

"Do cybercrime investigators see many dead bodies?"

"Actually, yes, I've been called to a few scenes." And he couldn't count how many pictures he'd seen while working on cases.

"Oh. I'm sorry."

He smiled and walked into the bathroom. The smell of chlorine and bleach hung in the air.

"They finally cleaned up yesterday." She shivered. "Come on, Ethan, let's get the hell out of here."

She could tell he wanted to stay, but instead, he nodded and followed her out of the bathroom, and up the stairs to her apartment.

As she opened the door, nerves tickled her stomach. No one had been in her apartment, especially a man, and especially not one that she was extremely attracted to.

"Nice place."

"Thanks."

"How long have you been here?"

"A month."

"Is all this furniture and stuff yours?"

"No, the apartment comes fully furnished, which works out well for me." She walked over to the kitchen. "Do you want a drink?"

"Sure."

"Water, milk, beer, or wine?"

"Beer."

She felt his eyes on her as she turned, opened the fridge and pulled out a bottle of beer. She popped the top, turned and met his gaze. Butterflies danced in her stomach as his eyes locked on hers. His six-foot-two body seeming out of place among her small, dainty things. His sex appeal filled every inch the room.

Damn, he had a way of knocking her off her game and clouding her thoughts.

She forced herself to look away and poured a hefty glass of wine. She crossed the room and handed him the beer.

He held the bottle up and raised his eyebrows. "A stout beer. Nice." He sipped. "I was expecting a light beer, or one of those diet beers that taste like water."

"I take my alcohol seriously."

"I like it."

She grinned. "Your approval means everything to me, Ethan."

"So Jolene, what brought you to Berry Springs? And let's be honest now."

She sat on the couch. "A job."

He sat next to her. "The job where you pulled a gun on my best friend?"

"One and the same."

He opened his mouth to say something before she interrupted.

"No, Ethan, you promised me that I don't have to rat anyone out. Besides, you guys arrested everyone involved, except for me, of course." She sipped. "And I know what you're wondering. I was simply hired to hide some of their assets, that's it. I wasn't involved in anything that they did, or were planning to do."

He rested his elbows on his knees and looked at her. "But Jolene, you *were* involved. Maybe not directly, but you were."

She looked down for a moment.

"Okay, so we won't talk about that. Tell me then, you spend your life moving from town to town, assuming new identities, for jobs?"

"That's right."

"And this makes you happy?"

"It makes me money, Ethan. A lot."

"How much?"

"Enough to stay at The Plaza."

He laughed. "What good is all this money going to do for you when you go to jail?"

"I don't plan on going to jail because you're going to wipe my slate clean once I deliver Packer to you."

"Exactly. Just get me the names of his associates." He turned toward her, his eyes narrowed. "I don't want you getting too deep in this, Jolene."

She opened her mouth to deliver another smartass response, but stopped. There was a sudden change in him, in his eyes, his voice—something protective.

He sipped his beer and changed the subject. "Is your family back in Chicago?"

"Yes."

"And?"

"And what?"

"Are you close? Brothers or sisters?"

"I have four brothers, a drug-addicted mom, and I have no idea who my father is."

He blew out a breath. "Wow." His voice softened. "I'm sorry. I'm sorry I asked."

"Don't be, it's okay. Last I heard my mom was in jail—drug charges and my brothers are following in her footsteps. I'm glad I got out."

"Do you have any communication with them at all?"

"Nope."

He looked down.

She looked at him for a long moment. "If I had to guess, you're very close with your family."

"Yes, I am."

She smiled. "That's great. I... I would have loved that but it just wasn't in the cards for me, I guess. And that's okay. It is what it is."

"It could still be in the cards for you."

She smiled and nodded.

He sipped and looked around the room, his gaze landing on a small picture on the end table. "You said just brothers, right?"

"Right."

"So who's the little girl in the photo?"

Her eyes shot to the framed picture, her body tensed.

"Whoa, why so jumpy all of a sudden?"

She pushed off the couch. "I'm going to grab some water. You need anything?"

As she walked across the room, he stood and followed her. "I need to know why that little girl made you so jumpy."

Buying some time, she grabbed a glass from the cabinet. "It's… she's a friend."

"You have a seven-year-old buddy?"

"She's eleven now and yes."

Not willing to let the conversation go, he leaned against the counter and raised his eyebrows.

"God, you're nosy."

"Blame it on the occupation."

She leaned against the counter across from him and met his gaze. Finally, she sighed, and said, "Her name is Allison. She's from Kansas."

"And how did you meet Allison from Kansas?"

Nerves tingled through her body; her anxiety began slowly creeping up. She took a deep sip of her wine, set it down, picked up a napkin and began nervously twisting it. She looked at Ethan, who was giving her his undivided attention.

Her voice softened. "She's why I got out of cybertheft." She took a deep breath and began the story. "Her parents were victims of a scam I was associated with. A big scam. One of the biggest I'd been involved with actually. Her dad was a doctor and her mom owned a small business. Anyway, my partners bled them dry." She looked down. "Stole every penny out of their savings accounts. Out of everything."

She looked out the window, her eyes filled with sadness and regret. She inhaled. "I found out that shortly after, the dad had lost his job, and her mom's business went under. I also found out that a portion of the money in their account had been saved to purchase Allison a pair of prosthetic legs. She'd lost them in a horrible boating accident when she was just a toddler."

The room was silent.

"When I found that out, I knew I couldn't do it anymore. Not ever again." She took another sip, her eyes brightening. "So I reimbursed their savings account, by twice the amount, purchased two top-of-the-line prosthetic legs for Allison, and I've set her up a college fund. I wrote the family a letter of apology, anonymously of course, and Allison writes to me—to a random PO box I gave her— and sends me pictures and stuff." Before she could compose herself, her eyes filled with tears. "She's a very special little girl." She shook her head, shaking the tears and emotions away. "So there's your story, Ethan."

"I…" his voice cracked. "I… wow, that's a hell of a story, Jolene."

"I still feel guilty every single day."

"You shouldn't. Everyone makes mistakes and you more than made up for it."

She looked down. "I hope so."

She suddenly felt uncomfortable, suffocated. She wasn't sure why, but had an idea that it had something to do with the man standing across the counter from her. She couldn't remember the last time she'd gotten emotional in front of a man, especially one that she was attracted to. Extremely attracted to.

She felt vulnerable, exposed. And she didn't like it.

"Anyway, I'll let you know when I get something on Packer."

Picking up on her cue, he set down his beer—his sexy, penetrating eyes still locked on hers. "You're not a bad person, Jolene."

She pushed away from the counter. "I'll show you out."

And with that, she led the only man she'd been attracted to in years out her door.

Debbie blew out a breath as she rounded the corner. A bright moon lit her path as she stepped onto the narrow sidewalk that ran along the outskirts of the park. A cold gust of wind whipped through her hair and she quickly zipped up her jacket.

What a night.

What a hell of a night.

Her stomach sank of embarrassment as she thought back on the dinner with Ethan. Who the hell would've known it would have been so awkward? She'd had more than a few first dates in her life and all of them were, what she considered, successful. Men drooled over her, clung to her every word, and always, *always*, tried to take her home at the end of the night.

No, first dates had never been a problem for Debbie.

As she walked along the edge of the park, she felt angry. Maybe not angry so much, but frustrated, definitely.

She replayed their conversation over and over in her head. What the hell was wrong with him? She was her usual, charming self and she'd even worn her signature style—a low-cut blouse.

She rolled her eyes and shook her head. Whatever. Maybe she'd never see him again.

The wind sent a chill up her spine as she looked around. She'd passed the play area of the park and was now walking along the edge of the woods. A cloud drifted over the moon, blocking out the light.

And suddenly, just belong the tree line, a faint *snick* of a twig.

Her heart skittered as she paused. She looked around—she was all alone.

Another sound, this one the rustle of dead leaves.

Get the hell out of here.

She gripped her purse straps and started to take a step when a burst of movement flashed beside her. Before she could react, a black bag was yanked over her head and a hand slammed over her nose and mouth.

Panic seized her as she tried to inhale, her chest squeezing for air. She clawed, scratched and swiped at her attacker as she was dragged into the woods. Twigs and branches sliced at her legs as she was pulled further in. She forced herself to open her eyes, only to see total darkness.

She was dropped to the ground; the hand released from her mouth and was swiftly replaced with the cold pressure of a blade to her throat.

"You scream, I slice your throat."

Tears filled her eyes; her body trembled in fear.

"You move, I slice your throat."

She held her breath and forced herself to lay like a dead fish. A gutted, dead fish.

Her heart raced in her chest and despite the cool

ground, beads of sweat dotted her forehead underneath the black bag that clung to her head.

In a low, gravelly voice, her attacker knelt down close to her ear. "Are you working with Ethan?"

Her eyes bugged under the bag. *What the fuck?*

She started to squirm but froze when the tip of the blade pierced her skin.

"I'm not going to ask again."

She opened her mouth—which felt like it was stuffed with thirty cotton balls—and in as loud a voice as her fear would allow, she said, "No, no. Please."

"Don't lie to me."

"I'm not... I don't... please."

"What did he tell you?"

She shook her head, tears running like a river over her face. "Please, I don't know what you're talking about. Please, please, let me go." As the words wept out, she was overrun with panic. Her heart hammered, her breath suffocating. As the adrenaline and panic began to flood her veins, all common sense escaped her and she pushed herself up in an attempt to flee.

The knife plunged into her side.

Her body froze, her breath caught.

As she opened her mouth to scream, she felt the warm blood spreading over her skin, and pain of the knife plunging into her again, and again.

CHAPTER 17

"JAMESON HERE."

"Jameson, it's Walker."

"Hey, Dean, what's up."

"Did I wake you?"

"What else do you think I'd be doing at five in the morning?"

"Well, you're about to be knee-deep in a dead body."

A moment ticked by before he heard the phone rustle against the sheets. Jameson cleared his throat. "What? I think I misheard you."

"I just got a call about a body found in the park."

"Are you serious?"

"No, I enjoy calling you at five in the morning and cracking jokes about murdered victims."

Pause. "Well, *shit*. Alright, I'll be there as quick as I can. Where're you at?"

"Just pulled in."

"Alright, see you soon."

Dean shoved his patrol car into park and got out. The early morning fog danced across the parking lot, snaking in and out of the trees in the distance. Barely light enough to see, he reached into his console and retrieved a flashlight.

"Hey. Hey, officer."

Dean turned to see an older man emerge from the bathrooms.

"Are you Harold?"

The man nodded and wiped his mouth, his face as pale as the hood of Dean's car. "Sorry, I, uh, got sick."

Seeing dead body will do that to a man. "Understandable. You okay?"

He nodded. "Yes, sir. Wow, you got here quick. It seemed like I just called it in."

"I was close by. You said the body is in the woods?"

"Yes, this way."

They fell into step side-by-side.

"What time did you discover the body?"

"Right before I called, literally, under a minute after. I was out for my morning walk, uh, like I do every morning, and decided to cut through the woods on my way back home."

Dean nodded as he listened. It never ceased to amaze him how much information someone voluntarily divulged when speaking with a man of the law.

"I, uh, I almost stepped on her. Right on her face."

Which means he'd probably danced all over the crime scene, dammit.

"Did you see anyone else around?"

"No."

"What about in the park?"

"No."

"Cars? Parked cars?"

"No, not that I can recall. I'm usually the only person out this early in the morning... my body clock wakes me up at four every morning. Old age, I guess."

"And you walk every morning?"

He nodded enthusiastically. "Oh, yes sir, absolutely."

"Good for you. That'll keep you young." Dean shot him a smile, to ease him.

"That's the intention."

"So you walked yesterday morning, then?"

They stepped into the woods. "Yes, sir."

"See anyone? Anything abnormal?"

"Not that I can recall."

"Cars? Parked or driving by?"

"Gosh, I don't think so." He momentarily broke his stride. "It's... she's just beyond that bush."

"Okay, stay here, please. I'll be right back."

"Yes, sir."

Dean flicked on his flashlight and scanned the ground, looking for any obvious evidence that he needed to avoid, before he walked up to the body.

"*Son of a bitch,*" he muttered as he reached for his radio. "Dispatch, I need additional units in the area sent to my location."

Crackle, crackle. "10-4, do we need to contact CID?"

"Already did, but we'll need the ME."

"10-4, additional units will be there shortly."

He slipped the radio back onto his belt and turned to see Jameson striding through the brush.

Harold took a few steps back as Jameson passed by

him, walked up to Dean, and looked down at the body in the grass.

The thick fog slithered like snakes across her body, sprawled out on the wet ground. A black bag wrapped over her head, with long blonde hair spilling out of the sides. Circles of dried blood drenched her white silk blouse, marking multiple stab wounds. One leg lay straight, the other bent backward at the knee like a check mark. Her black jeans were speckled with mud and dirt. One red high-heel hung by her bright pink toenail, the other in the grass a few feet away.

"Son of a bitch."

"My thoughts exactly."

"You call for reinforcements?"

Dean nodded.

"Alright, let's see who she is."

Jameson slipped on a pair of latex gloves, tossed Dean a pair, then tiptoed over to the front of the body. He kneeled down and carefully pulled the bag over her chin, revealing her face.

His eyes rounded. "Oh, *shit*." He looked up at Dean. "Debbie."

Dean raised his eyebrows in shock.

Jameson blew out an exhale. "Dammit."

Dean looked down at the woman he'd played darts with less than forty-eight hours earlier. A young woman, with her whole life ahead of her. He shook his head. "Unbelievable. Looks like she hasn't been here too long."

"No, my guess would be it happened sometime last night. And based on her outfit, she wasn't jogging."

"Or working. She looks a little too dressed up for work."

Jameson nodded and a moment slid by before Dean addressed the elephant in the room. "So… we've got two dead bodies now. Both stabbed."

In deep thought, Jameson nodded and said, "It's about to blow up, Walker."

"It sure is."

Jameson glanced over at Harold who was incessantly fidgeting with his coat zipper. "Is that who called her in?"

Dean nodded.

"Alright, I'm going to go chat with him."

Car doors slammed in the distance. Loud voices and swift steps carried through the brisk morning breeze, turning the bleak morning into a circus.

"Hey, Dean."

Rookie Officer Jasper Hayes jogged through the brush, followed closely by the Medical Examiner Jessica Heathrow.

"Hayes, I need you to secure the scene immediately. And who the hell else is out there?"

"Fucking media." Jessica popped a rubber band off her wrist and began pulling back her wild, red hair. Born and raised in Berry Springs, Jessica was known for her ball-busting attitude, foul mouth, and keen instincts at a crime scene.

"Are you serious?"

"Yep. Must've heard it over the radio."

"Dammit."

Jessica set down her bag, pulled out a pair of gloves and booties. "Tell me Jameson didn't trek all over the damn body."

Dean grinned. "Okay, I won't."

Jameson and Jessica's working relationship was legendary in Berry Springs. One moment they would be screaming in each other's faces, and the next, working side-by-side to solve a murder. Dean often wondered if there was more to the relationship than meets the eye.

She rolled her eyes, slipped on her booties and walked up to the body.

Her mouth gaped open. "Holy shit. That's Diner Debbie, isn't it?"

He nodded.

Eyes bugging, she glanced over her shoulder at Jameson, who was still interviewing Harold, and then squatted down next to the victim. "*Son. Of. A. Bitch.*"

"That seems to be the general consensus."

She looked up at Dean. "And stabbed. Shit man, she was stabbed just like Chase Martinez."

"You'll be the one to determine cause of death, but it appears that way."

She looked around. "Purse? Cell phone?"

"Nope."

Jameson walked up and looked down at Jessica. "That was quick. Didn't expect you to show up until after the all-you-can-eat pancake special at Donny's Diner."

"Well, your dad's house is just around the block, so…"

Jameson grinned at the quip. "Always a pleasure to see you, Miss Heathrow."

"You too, dickhead." She sat back on her heels and looked up. "Chase and now Debbie. Looks like you got a hell of a case on your hands."

His eyes clouded as he nodded. "Let's get pictures first, and then you can have your way with her."

"You got it."

Dean slipped a pair of booties over his combat boots. "Alright guys, I'm going to check for tracks. The killer had to leave somewhere." He glanced over his shoulder, "And Hayes, hurry up. We need this scene secured ASAP. The last thing we need is the damn media walking up on us."

"They're already in the parking lot."

"All the more reason to bust your ass, don't you think?"

"Yes, sir."

He looked at Jameson. "I'll have Jonas look for her car."

"Good, and after we wrap up here we'll head to the diner. Maybe someone saw her last night."

"Sounds like a plan."

"Hey, Detective Jameson." Wide-eyed, the waitress tossed a coaster on the table and leaned forward. She whispered, "Is it true?"

Jameson took a deep breath and glanced around Frank's Bar. It was slow for a weeknight, which is exactly what he'd hoped for. Only a couple playing a game of pool in the back, and two girls, clad in bejeweled cowboy boots sat at the bar sipping their Jack and Cokes, no doubt out on the prowl. He'd usually be inclined to go talk to them after a few drinks, but not tonight. Tonight, he was more inclined to tell them to get home, stay there and lock their doors until he found whoever the hell was stabbing people to death.

"You know I can't get into that, Linda."

"I know, I know." She hesitated. "But *Debbie*. I mean

Debbie! Is it true that it's her? I mean, it's all over the news, and that's what everyone's saying. *Everyone's* saying it's her, Detective."

He began to regret agreeing to take a quick break from work to grab dinner.

"Hey, Linda."

Dean, followed closely by Jonas, walked up and sank into the chairs across from Jameson.

Linda's eyes lit up at the mere sight of Dean. "Hey, Dean." She smiled, gazing at him for a moment, and then tore her eyes away. "Hey, Jonas. God, you guys look exhausted." She looked back at Jameson. "Sorry for pestering you. Anyway, what can I get y'all to drink?"

"Iced tea."

She raised her eyebrows, shocked at his alcohol-free order.

He smiled. "It's going to be a long night."

Dean leaned back in his chair. "It sure is. And in that case, I'll take a beer, please, whatever you've got on tap."

She smiled. "You got it. And for you, Jonas?"

"Hell, I'll get a beer too."

"Be right back."

Jameson rubbed his head in exhaustion. It was seven in the evening—exactly fourteen hours since they'd found Debbie's body—and they had been running nonstop all day.

"Ethan's on his way."

Jonas cocked an eyebrow. "Are we involving the FBI?"

"Hell, no. We can do this without them. He's just meeting up for a beer."

It was no secret that the Berry Springs PD—or any police department for that matter—didn't take kindly to the FBI sweeping in, taking over, and stepping on their toes. It was a constant pissing match with no end in sight.

Dean nodded. "It will be good to get his perspective, though."

"Absolutely. He's smart as shit, and we could use an extra brain to bounce things off of."

"Here you go boys. One iced tea and two beers."

"Make that three, please." Ethan walked up, tossed his keys on the table and sat down.

"You got it." The waitress scribbled on her notepad and walked away.

"Hey, Ethan."

A line of concern drew in between his eyebrows. "What's going on? You guys look like shit."

"I guess you haven't heard?"

Linda slid an ice-cold beer across the table as an old Merle Haggard song played from the jukebox. "Here's your beer. I'll give you a second to look over the menu."

"Thanks." He sipped and turned back to the group. "Heard what?"

"Debbie, you know, Diner Debbie?"

"Yeah…"

"She was murdered last night."

He choked on his beer and broke into a coughing fit.

Dean slapped him on the back. "Shit, man, you okay?"

He swallowed and swiped his forearm across his mouth. "*What?*"

"Debbie was killed last night."

His eyes rounded, shock slid across his face. "I was with her last night."

Jameson set down his tea and leaned forward. "What?"

"Yeah." His stomach began churning. "Yeah, we went to dinner."

"What the fuck? Are you serious? When? Where?"

He inhaled lightly, trying to calm his racing heart. "To that barbecue joint, off the square."

Dean and Jameson exchanged glances. "We found her car parked on the square. Did she ride with you?"

"No, we met at the restaurant. When we were leaving, she said she'd parked her car on the square because she planned on running into the diner before going home for the evening. She wanted to walk."

"Whoa, what time was this?"

He thought for a moment. "We finished up around nine or so." He shook his head. "Hang on a minute, what the hell happened? Where was she found? When?"

Linda walked up. "Y'all ready to order?"

They rattled off their orders and after the waitress walked away, Jameson quietly gave Ethan the details of the murder.

Ethan leaned back and blew out a breath. "So then, that makes sense. She'd have to walk by the park to get to the square." He shook his head. "I can't believe this."

Dean cleared his throat. "You know we'll have to verify your whereabouts after, just for the record, of course."

"Of course. I'll give you full access to the GPS records of my phone, and I'm sure I'm on the camera getting gas and swinging through the ATM."

He wasn't sure why but he left out the part about visiting Jolene. He didn't want to deal with the onslaught of questions about their relationship, but more than that, he didn't need to bring any unnecessary attention to her, considering her circumstances. If it came down to it, he'd provide her as an alibi, but only if it were absolutely necessary.

"Thanks."

"No problem."

Linda delivered their burgers, with Dean's having a noticeably heftier amount of all the fixings, and a large basket of fries.

Jonas rolled his eyes. "Ever get sick of women bending over backwards for you, man?"

"I never get sick of a woman bending over backwards." He winked.

Although his stomach was uneasy, Ethan bit into his burger. "Do you guys have any suspects?"

Jameson swallowed his bite and took a sip of tea. "No, not yet. We interviewed everyone at the diner and spoke with her family of course. Everyone said they weren't aware of any enemies, and were completely shocked of course. She wasn't seeing anyone; no disgruntled exes, nothing."

Dean sipped his beer, set it down. "Her purse and cell phone were gone."

"Robbery?"

"We're looking into it."

"Pretty vicious robbery. I mean, her head was bagged. Why not just take her purse and run?"

Dean nodded; obviously the same thought had run through his mind. "Furthermore, if it were a robbery, why didn't they take her car, too?"

Jonas, who had been abnormally quiet, asked, "So she had no enemies, exes, etcetera, but what about love interests? It's no secret that almost every guy in town had the hots for her. What about someone who was obsessed or something?"

Just then, the front door swung open, blowing in dead leaves that had collected on the sidewalk.

Adrenalin flushed Greg's cheeks as he stood in the doorway and looked around. His gaze landed on Detective Jameson.

"What the fuck," Jameson muttered as he watched Greg stomp across the bar, beelining it for their table.

Ethan looked over his shoulder and his back stiffened, his senses shifting to alert. He'd seen plenty of pissed off men in his line of work, and Greg was one pissed off dude.

"Detective." Greg walked up to the front of the table, fists clenched, his breath short.

"Greg, what can I do for ya?"

"Is it true?"

"Is what true?"

"Is she dead? Is…" his voice shook with emotion. "Was Debbie murdered?"

Jameson shot Dean a look that said *I knew we should've stayed in the office*, before looking back at Greg. "I can't really get into that."

"The hell you can't." His voice pitched and the few people in the bar began to take notice.

Dean scooted back his chair discreetly—easier to jump to his feet if the situation called for it. "What's got you so worked up, Greg?"

"I, uh… I just wanted to know if it's true." His eyes darted across the table and landed on Ethan. "Who're you?"

"Ethan Veech."

Greg's eyes widened. "*Ethan Veech?*"

Ethan cocked an eyebrow. "Have we met?"

The flush on Greg's cheeks slowly made its way down to his neck. His eyes bugged. "Are you… didn't you go on a date with her? You did, *didn't you?*"

As Ethan opened his mouth to respond, Greg lunged forward, sending the drinks flying off the table, and grabbed Ethan by the throat. Chaos erupted as Ethan shook out of his hold and surged to his feet, his chair flying backward.

Like a flash of lightning, Dean leapt over the table, tackled Greg, flipped him on his back and secured him in handcuffs in seconds flat.

CHAPTER 18

JOLENE GLANCED AT the clock—nine o'clock—and sat back on her heels and looked around. One suitcase packed with clothes, another open and empty on the floor, and a half-drunk glass of red wine.

She took a deep breath.

Somewhere during the restless night's sleep after Ethan had left her apartment the night before, she'd decided that it was time to leave the beautiful, small town of Berry Springs, Arkansas.

As soon as her deal with Ethan was complete, of course.

She wasn't sure what it was about him that had gotten her so emotional, but she didn't like it. Sure, she'd been in fleeting relationships here and there, but not many. Even if she wanted to get close to someone, her job wouldn't allow for it.

So what the hell had gotten her all worked up about Ethan? Maybe it was his thick, chiseled body that made her feel safe and protected. Maybe it was his hazel eyes and the little gold flakes in them. Maybe it was the way her stomach did a little dance every time he was around. Maybe it was the look he'd given her, standing in front of her hotel room after he'd saved her life. Yes, it was all those things, but above all, it was the way she felt when she was with him. An indescribable magnetic pull that gripped her whole body and turned her brain to mush. A pull that made her want nothing else than to feel the weight of his body on top of hers.

So what did she decide to do about it? Get as far away from him as possible.

It would never work.

As she pushed off the floor, her phone rang.

"Hello?"

"Hey, it's Dylan."

"Hey, what's up?"

"Good news, I've made some progress on that little favor you asked of me."

"Perfect."

"Someone will be in touch with you soon."

Pause. "What do you mean someone will be in touch with me? I just need the names of known associates."

"Well, sweetheart, it wasn't that easy. Believe me, it was hell getting as far as I have. I'm telling you, Slade Packer is protected. Heavily."

She should have known it wouldn't have been that easy, and now, she had a feeling things were about to get even more complicated.

"So I just sit around until someone contacts me?"

"Yep, that's my understanding. Soon, too. That's all I know." Muffled voices sounded through the phone. "Hey, I gotta go. Talk soon."

"Okay, thanks. Bye."

Jolene tossed her phone on the couch and tried to ignore the pit in her stomach.

❧

"Need some more water?"

Pale as a ghost, Greg glanced up and shook his head.

"Alright." Dean leaned back in the chair, across the table. The bright fluorescent light of the interview room reflected off the sheen of sweat coating Greg's skin, and the slight green ring around his mouth had Jameson eyeing the trash can across the room.

It was apparent that Greg was at least five or six drinks from being sober.

After the scuffle at Frank's Bar, Dean could've just given Greg a verbal warning and kicked him out, but considering how worked up Greg had been about Debbie's murder, he decided to shake him out a bit.

He glanced at the two-way mirror where Jameson sat hidden on the other side. They'd decided against Jameson talking to Greg, in case he started to catch on that he was being interviewed for more than just the scuffle. With Dean interviewing him, Greg assumed he was being brought in about the bar fight and nothing regarding the recent murder.

"Greg, have you been drinking tonight?"

Greg twisted the white Styrofoam cup in his sweaty hands. "A little."

"How much is a little?"

"A few beers."

"A few?"

Greg shrugged and Dean started to push out of his chair. "Alright then, I'll go get the breathalyzer and…"

"Wait. Alright, I've had, like, six beers."

Six probably meant ten. "Celebrating something? Somewhere?"

Greg's body tensed. "No, uh, just drinking."

"Alone?"

"Yeah."

"Where?"

"My apartment."

"Is that where you heard about Debbie?"

His eyes flashed with emotion. "Yeah."

"Who told you?"

"My buddy, Paul. Sent me a text."

Dean scribbled in his notebook. "What did Paul say?"

"That he heard Debbie had been killed in the park."

Dean clenched his jaw. Damn leaks.

"And where did you get your information that led you to believe she and Ethan Veech had gone on a date?"

"I heard her say it. On the phone."

"When?"

"The night before last."

"Where?"

"Outside the diner."

"Where were you?"

"Sitting in my truck."

"Eavesdropping?"

"Yeah, I guess."

Dean had established the rapid-fire question and answer at this point, so he dug in.

"Why did you lunge at Ethan?"

Greg shrugged and looked down.

"Jealous?"

No response.

"Were you and Debbie friends?"

Greg shifted in his seat. "Yeah."

"Just friends?"

Greg didn't respond and Dean leaned forward, sensing there was going to be much more to this story.

"Were you more than friends, Greg?"

No response.

"Were you romantically involved with Debbie?"

Silence.

"Intimately?"

Color flushed on Greg's pasty cheeks. Bingo.

"So, yes?"

"I, uh…" Greg nervously pulled his hands down into his lap, and then back up on the table, then back down again. "Uh, we had been."

"Had been intimate?"

"Yes."

"When?"

"A few nights ago."

Dean glanced up at the mirror, then back at Greg. He was shocked Greg hadn't realized he was being interviewed about Debbie's murder. Maybe he'd had more than ten beers.

He went in for the kill. "Greg where were you last night between seven p.m. and eleven p.m.?"

Greg's head shot up, his eyes rounded. "*What?*"

"Where were you last night between seven and eleven?"

His voice cracked. "I stopped by the B&B for a bit."

"Barb's B&B?"

"That's right."

"Why?"

"I'm the cook there and I swung by to see if Barb needed anything."

That would be easy to verify. "Okay, then what?"

"And then went home to my apartment."

"Alone?"

His mouth opened, his eyes grew to the size of golf balls. "I want a lawyer."

Dammit.

Just then, a knock on the door and Jonas poked his head in. "Dean, can I talk to you for a minute?"

Dean glanced at Greg before pushing his chair back and meeting Jonas outside. As he pulled the door closed, Jameson joined them.

"What's up?"

Jonas shuffled through a stack of papers. "I just got the dump from the phone company."

"Debbie's phone?"

"Right." He pulled out a few pieces of paper with several highlights. "In light of this evening's activities," he cast a look toward Greg, "I cross referenced Greg's numbers and, check it out, they'd been texting frequently the last few weeks." He handed Jameson the paper. "The last text she'd received was from him, the evening she was killed."

Dean leaned in and looked at the paper. "Eight in the evening."

"Right."

Jameson looked up. "About an hour before her estimated time of death."

Jonas raised his eyebrows. "Exactly."

CHAPTER 19

ETHAN ROLLED TO a stop in front of the bed and breakfast, clicked off his headlights, and turned off the engine. Thick cloud cover blackened the already dark night. The two porch lights that flanked the front door twinkled like flames against the dark house. The B&B was officially closed for business until the murder of Chase Martinez was solved. And only God knew how long that would take.

He glanced up at the third floor where a low light and the flicker of a television shone through the window. She was awake.

After the hoopla at Frank's Bar, Ethan had followed the boys down to the station where they'd interviewed his red-headed, drunken attacker. Ethan was still unsure why the hell the little punk had taken a swing at him, but he had no doubt that Dean and Jameson were on it. And after two cups of the station's coffee that could burn a hole in a man's gut, he was wired. Restless.

And Jolene was on his mind.

It was just after ten o'clock and his fingers anxiously

tapped the steering wheel as he contemplated if he should get out of his truck. He'd hate to wake her if she was sleeping, but on the other hand, he didn't take her for a girl who went to bed early.

After another moment of hesitation, his desire just to see her beautiful face won out and he pushed out of his truck. A cool breeze, carrying with it the sweet scent of rain, swept past his skin.

Crisp leaves danced across his feet as he walked up the narrow pathway to the porch. The old wood planks creaked as he walked up the steps and pushed the button marked *Gable, Anna*.

A second ticked by.

He pushed it again.

"Yes?"

"Hey, it's Ethan."

Pause. "Hey." Pause. "Come on up." He waited a moment before the *buzz* of the door unlocked and he pushed it open. The house was silent, not even the low hum of a TV, or the *tick, tick, tick* of a clock.

He began walking up the old wooden staircase and a sudden unease swept over him. Why?

Thunder sounded faintly in the distance, a polite announcement of an impending storm.

He paused at the second-floor landing, and glanced into the room where Chase had been murdered. He had to stop himself from going into the room, to take another look around.

He stepped onto the third floor and stopped. A small, white envelope leaned up against the door to Jolene's apartment. He looked from side-to-side, then down the staircase before picking it up. The envelope had *Anna Gable* typed on the front.

Her door opened.

"Hey." Wearing yoga pants, a black tank top, no bra, and a smile, Jolene looked at the envelope in his hands. "What's that?"

He quickly tore his eyes away from her chest and smiled. "Hey. This was in front of your door."

She plucked it from his hands and frowned. "Huh. Weird." With her eyes locked on the envelope, she left the door open and turned—an invitation that he gladly accepted. As she walked to the living room, his eyes fell to her behind. Her perky, round, feminine ass. He felt a tingle in his pants and immediately shook the thought out of his head. God, what was with him tonight?

She set the envelope on the table. "To what do I owe this pleasure?"

"Can't a guy just stop by to say hi?"

She grinned. "In my experience, no."

"In that case I'll take a drink."

"Beer, wine, milk or water?"

"Beer."

She walked to the kitchen and his gaze landed on the two open suitcases on the floor. "Going somewhere?"

"Eventually."

"When?"

"As soon as this little deal of ours is over."

A sudden realization of their separate lives washed over him. Would he ever see her again after he left Berry Springs? Would he even know where to find her? The thought made his stomach sink, followed by a sudden feeling of desperation to hang onto her, tightly. For even just one night. Their eyes met, and for fear of exposing his thoughts, he quickly looked away, his gaze shifting to the envelope.

"Aren't you going to open that?"

She pulled two beers from the fridge and popped the tops. "Of course."

"Here you go."

"Thanks." He took a sip and they both stared down at the paper on the table.

"Well?"

She picked it up and sank onto the couch.

"Maybe you won a million dollars."

"I don't need a million dollars."

"I'll take it then."

He noticed her nerves as she carefully pried open the flap and pulled out a white piece of paper. Ethan stepped forward and leaned over as she unfolded it.

TEN PM, TOMORROW, DEVIL'S COVE.

Her eyes rounded as she looked up at him.

He plucked the paper from her hand. "No name."

She took a deep breath.

"By your expression, I'm guessing you know who it's from?"

She nodded and pushed off the couch. "I've got a pretty good idea." She put her hands on her hips and turned to him. "You said you wanted Packer, right?"

His eyebrows shot up. "You think Packer is *meeting you*? This is from him?"

"Possibly."

"Whoa, whoa, whoa, Jolene, I only asked you to get the names of the people who work for him, not to meet him for Christ's sake." He grabbed the envelope from the table and turned it over. Engraved in the lower right corner were the letters *S.P.*

"S.P., Slade Packer." He began pacing. "Where's Devil's Cove?"

"It's at the lake, a few miles from here."

"It's a public area?"

"No, you have to hike a pretty steep trail to get to it. It's a small cove with cliffs dropping down to the lake. Wooded."

He paused, his steely eyes locked on hers. "You're not going."

She cocked her head. "Oh yeah? Says who?"

He walked over, inches from her face. His eyes narrowed. "I say."

She laughed and sarcastically said, "Oh, okay, *yes sir*."

His jaw clenched. "I'm serious, you're not going."

"First, yes, I am. Second, do you seriously think Packer himself would be meeting me? I'm sure it's some messenger or something."

He tossed the envelope to her. "It's too dangerous."

She looked down at the paper, her brows furrowed. "S.P. doesn't necessarily mean it's from Slade."

He rolled his eyes.

"Maybe that's a coincidence. It could just be someone delivering the list of names to me."

"What did you ask for, exactly? What did you tell your contact you needed?"

"The list, the names of his associates, and anything on Bia. That's it."

"Not to meet with Packer personally?"

"No, I promise."

He took a sip of his beer and gazed out the window in deep thought. "You have a good point, then. Why would Packer hand deliver his own associates? Doesn't add up. Is it possible that it's from someone else entirely? About something else?"

She shook her head. "I don't think so."

He walked to her front door and pulled it open, glancing at the hall ceiling. "No cameras inside, huh?"

"No."

"She should really rethink that." He pulled the door closed.

"Considering the events of a few days ago, I'm sure she will."

He crossed the living room. "And considering those events, you're not going." He paused. "There's something else I haven't told you."

The look on his face made her take a step back. "What?"

"There's been another murder?"

"*What?*"

"A stabbing, in the park."

She covered her mouth. "Oh, my God, Ethan. Do they think it's the same person?"

"Not sure, yet. But it appears that way, from the outside looking in."

"Who was it?"

"A girl named Debbie, she worked at the diner."

She raised her eyebrows. "The girl that was texting you when we were in New York?"

He nodded.

She shook her head. "I can't believe this."

"Exactly. Back to my point, you're not going."

She stared blankly at him.

"Jolene, you're not going."

Thunder boomed outside the window, followed by a flash of lightning.

They stood in the middle of the living room a few feet apart, the electricity building in the air.

She looked at him with those big, brown eyes; her hair pulled back in a messy ponytail. The dim light of the table lamp outlined her curvy body, sending a surge of... something through him. A mixture of emotions—attraction, lust, nerves and anticipation for what he knew he was about to do. But above all else, he felt a pull of protectiveness. To protect her. To keep her safe.

Reading his expression, her eyes widened, her face softened. As if she were forcing herself to say it, she whispered, "You can't tell me what to do, Ethan."

Another boom of thunder, this time rattling the windows before a loud *pop!* and then total darkness.

He blinked, allowing his eyes to adjust to the blackness. "You okay?"

"Yeah. I guess the electricity went out."

"Do you have any candles?"

"On the coffee table."

"Stay there, I'll get it." He slowly walked forward until the toe of his boot bumped the table. He felt around and grabbed the candle, and thank God, a lighter lying right next to it. As the candle caught, he set it back down on the table.

He turned to face her, inches from her face.

༚

Her heart raced as she looked up at him. Her feet felt frozen to the ground, her legs paralyzed. She could actually *feel* the sexual tension between them.

The rain began sprinkling on the roof, slow at first, then quickly turned into a deluge pouring outside the windows.

The candlelight danced across his face and her stomach tickled with anticipation.

His fierce eyes locked on hers and he slowly stepped forward, closing the inches between them. Her heart was a steady thudding now as she gazed up at all six-foot-two inches of his perfect body and face.

His expression awoke butterflies of nerves inside her.

He reached forward, tucking a strand of loose hair behind her ear. His finger lingered, before lightly trailing from her ear, along her jawline and down her neck, sending goosebumps running up her body. He stopped below her chin and lightly raised her face toward him.

Her breath caught as he looked into her eyes.

Kiss me, Ethan.

Take me.

As if reading her mind, his large hands cupped her face—her breath caught—and he leaned down and kissed her.

Her head spun, her thoughts clouded to total mush.

He had her. One hundred percent, he had her.

She wrapped her arms around his hard body, running her fingers down his back. In response to her touch, he kissed harder, passionately, greedily.

He pulled off her tank top and then in one, quick, fluid movement, picked her up, and she wrapped her legs around his waist. He turned toward the bedroom.

"Wait."

He pulled back, his eyes wide with surprise.

She smiled. "The candle."

He lowered her to where she could grab it, and then hastily carried her into the bedroom. She slid the candle on the dresser before he tossed her on the bed. His aggressiveness had her clenching her jaw in an animalistic frenzy of lust.

Take me, she thought, *take me, Ethan.* God, she wanted him so bad. More than she'd ever wanted anyone before in her life.

He undressed her, caressing her skin; the fire in his eyes driving her crazy. He straightened and pulled off his shirt, kicked off his boots and slid out of his pants.

Her mouth gaped open as she looked over his chiseled body, and then her eyes landed on his rock-hard...

Oh, my God.

The corner of his lip curled up—his confidence making him even *sexier.*

He crawled on top of her, wrapped his arm around her back and pulled her further up on the bed. She felt like a rag doll underneath him, willing to do whatever he asked.

She parted her lips in anticipation for his kiss but was left lingering when he edged down and took her nipple into his mouth. As his warm, wet tongue circled her breast, his hand swept down her ribcage, down her belly, and finally, between her legs.

She was already throbbing with desire when his finger swept across her clit. A shot of electricity burst through her system at the mere touch, followed by a rush of wetness. It had been so long.

He lightly ran his fingers over her inner lips, then brushed over her clit again. He was teasing her, and she liked it. She squirmed, her body screaming for him do it again. To touch it again.

He lightly bit her nipple and looked up from her breast, the candlelight dancing across his face. With his eyes locked on hers, he licked his finger and then trailed it back down her body, stopping on her swollen bud. This time, his wet finger slid over it as if he had all the time in the world. Slowly, gently rubbing circles around her, making her wetter with each stroke. She tipped her head back and groaned, the sensation running tingles all over her body. She dug her fingernails into his back as he rubbed, harder, faster, and she almost exploded when he inserted a finger deep inside her.

Thunder boomed outside, followed by a flash of lightning, monetarily illuminating the room. Her senses piqued.

Her skin prickled, the heat radiating from between her legs. She lost all perception of time, space, everything, as the sensation built and built. He laid his lips on hers and slid his tongue into her mouth as he inserted another finger, in, out, in, out, and then glided back onto her clit, wet with desire.

"Oh, *Ethan.*"

He rubbed faster.

"*Ethan.*"

Her body released into an explosion. She bucked, arched, fully giving in to the pleasure before melting into the bed in complete euphoria.

Her heart raced in her chest, her body throbbing from the orgasm. Disoriented, she opened her eyes and looked at him, the intensity and strength of the storm outside reflecting in his eyes.

"We're not done."

She cocked an eyebrow before he leaned down and began kissing her, again.

Before she knew it, she felt another rush of energy as she kissed him back.

His hard cock dangled above her as he whispered in her ear, "You ready?"

"*Yes.*"

He paused at her opening, her breath caught in anticipation, and then he plunged into her, her body tightening around him.

"*Oh, my God,*" she whispered.

A sheen of sweat coated his skin as he slowly slid in and out of her wetness, filling her with every inch of him. She greedily arched her back and pushed forward with each thrust, giving him all she had, too.

He ran his fingers through her hair as he kissed her and began to pick up his pace.

In, out, in, out, the sensation between her legs building with each thrust.

Faster, harder. His breathing became labored, his muscles tightened.

"Oh, Ethan."

Faster, harder, deeper.

"Say it again."

"Oh, *Ethan.*"

Thunder shook the windows.

"*Ethan.*"

As she released, again, he exploded himself into her at the same time.

He collapsed on top of her and for a moment, their hearts thudded in perfect rhythm. Eventually, he rolled over and looked at her, a smile crossing his face.

"Two, huh?"

She laughed and rolled her eyes. "Oh, *please.*"

He chuckled, lightly grabbed her hand and kissed the top.

Her heart swelled, and as the storm raged outside, she laid next to him, in a comfortable silence, trying to calm the storm of emotions raging through her body.

After a minute, he glanced over at the candle that was beginning to dim. "Do you have more candles?"

"No, actually, I don't."

He pushed up on his elbows. "Pack a bag, you're staying with me."

CHAPTER 20

"YOU SURE SEEM to do a lot of hacking for someone who's not a criminal."

He looked over his shoulder where Jolene was hunched over, peering at his computer screen.

After leaving her apartment, they'd picked up fast-food and drove through the dark, stormy night to the cabin, which thankfully, had electricity.

The sudden comfort between them sent a warm rush through his body and he leaned up and kissed her cheek, then turned back to the screen. "Look who's talking. An actual criminal."

"Yeah, but you work for the government."

"Well, I'm technically not right now."

"What do you mean?"

"I'm not logged in or using secure government sites. This is my personal computer. I learned my lesson last time I hacked into Packer's computer."

"I see. So what exactly are you doing?"

He scooted back, patted his knee. She sat.

"I'm going to see what I can find out about our little friend Bia, and see if my hunch is correct."

"That Packer has hired, or blackmailed him, to take control of our nukes." She rolled her eyes.

"I thought we talked about that attitude of yours."

She grinned.

"But yeah, I just want to see what I can find out." His fingers flew over the keyboard. As if he were talking to himself, he muttered, "I already pulled his government file, was able to get his cell phone information, and then traced that, and… I'm in."

"You're in what?"

"His personal computer. Well, one of them."

"No shit?"

"No shit. Now let's hope I don't get locked out immediately like I did with Packer."

She squinted and leaned forward. "What the hell are you looking it?"

"A shit-load of encrypted files."

"You can read that?"

"Kind of."

She sipped her wine. "God, you're a dork."

His fingers paused momentarily on the keyboard and he looked at her with a twinkle in his eye. "That's not what you were saying an hour ago." He held up two fingers and winked.

"You're so obnoxious." She grinned and drained her drink. "I'm getting more wine, need some?"

"Yes, please, ma'am."

She walked to the other side of the kitchen. "Now what? You're looking at a mess of encrypted files that you can't even read."

"Oh, I can read them. I just have to find the right program to decipher it. Wait a second…"

"What?"

"This is… no way."

She returned with two glasses of wine. "What?"

"This is… I don't recognize most of the code, but," he pointed to the screen, "these design patterns…" His mouth dropped as his eyes scanned the code. "This is a ransomware virus. Holy shit. A hard-core ransomware virus."

"What the hell is that?"

"Think of it like a virus that takes control of your computer system until you give the hacker whatever they want. You're locked out of everything, while they have access to everything." He clicked some more keys. "It's everywhere, but this is built differently than any other code I've seen."

Her eyes rounded. "You could be right. Packer hired him to build a virus to download into the NRC. Hold the nukes ransom."

"Right. But more than that, Bia could be using this for anything. *Anything.* Hell, he could sell this virus to terrorists. Holy shit." His fingers flew over the keyboard. "I've got to copy this."

"Shouldn't you call your FBI buddies right about now?"

Barely listening to her, he muttered, "Uh-huh, I will." Just then, the screen went black.

"*Dammit.*"

"What?"

"Got locked out." He yanked out his thumb drive. "But I think I got part of it copied."

"So now what?"

"Need to analyze it. Might be nothing. I'll need to spend

time looking it over." He scooted back in his chair and gazed up at Jolene. "But first, I need to make a phone call."

"Okay…"

He walked down the hall, plucked the phone from his coat pocket and dialed the number.

"Hello?"

"Jessica Heathrow?"

"You got her."

"Hey, it's Ethan Veech, FBI. We met a few weeks ago when I was in town working on the Stooges case."

"Oh, yeah! Hey, Ethan. Thanks for your help with that. How the hell are ya?"

"Good, am I calling too late?"

"No, I never sleep. Still working actually, even through this damned storm. What can I do for ya?"

"I need an envelope scanned for DNA."

She blew out a breath. "Stuff like that gets sent down to the state crime lab, you know. Takes a while."

"I need it as soon as possible. By tomorrow evening the latest."

"Dead bodies are my expertise, not pulling DNA off envelopes."

"But you can do it, right?"

"Technically, yeah, but if it's important, you'll want to send it to the lab. I don't want to be responsible for fucking it up."

"I trust you." But more than that, he knew that she was his only option to get it done in under twenty-four hours.

"Alright, I'll see what I can do. But I'm swimming in bodies down here. You know that, right?"

"How does three-hundred bucks sound?"

"Five."

"Four."

"Deal. Drop it off first thing in the morning and I'll have it to you before I go home for the day."

He grinned. "Nice doing business with you."

She laughed and hung up.

✍

"Hey, Jameson."

Jameson looked up from his computer screen and blinked while his eyes adjusted. He was on three hours of sleep and already back in the office before seven in the morning. Two back-to-back murders will do that to a detective.

"What's up?"

Jonas stepped into the office. "Your morning is about to get much more interesting." He laid a piece of paper on his desk. "Got the identity of the bones found in the lake."

He raised his eyebrows. With so much going on, he'd almost forgotten about the mystery bones.

"No shit? That was fast."

"Yeah, I was surprised, too." Jonas paused for effect. "Does the name Lisa Halstead ring a bell?"

He searched his memory and plucked the paper from his desk. "Yeah, rings a bell but…"

"The senator's daughter who went missing fifteen years ago."

"You're fucking kidding me."

"Nope. Remember, she was kidnapped and held for ransom, for like a million dollars or something, and when the deadline passed, she was never heard from again. Case went cold."

"*Shit.*"

"Yeah, exactly."

"Wasn't she from…"

"Missouri."

"That's right. And the FBI was all over it." He shook his head. "Wow, the media is going to go nuts. Is McCord in yet? He'll want to handle this one, I'm sure."

"Don't think so; his truck wasn't in the parking lot when I got here."

"I'll call him, then."

"Anything else happen with Greg last night?"

"No, he lawyered up pretty quick and we had nothing to hold him on. No crime in texting Debbie right before she was murdered."

"What did the text say?"

"Perry advised him against telling us," he shook his head. "So we've got to go through the phone company. Hoping to get it today."

"We still haven't found her cell phone or purse?"

"Nope."

"Damn."

"Yep. She's with Jessica right now, I told her to rush the autopsy."

"Has she even finished Chase Martinez's?"

"No. I'm expecting her report this morning on that one."

Jonas frowned. "A stabbing at the B&B; a stabbing in the park; and now the fifteen-year-old bones of the senator's daughter found in our lake. What the fuck?"

Jameson nodded and blankly looked at his email, in

deep thought. Then, suddenly the *ding* of a new email. "Speak of the devil."

"What?"

"Jessica's autopsy report."

"Morning, kids." Dean walked into the room looking as fresh and alert as he always did, even though Jameson knew he'd had about as much sleep as he had.

"Hey. Just got the autopsy report from Jessica regarding Chase Martinez."

Dean cocked an eyebrow. "Nice turnaround time."

"Yeah, two back-to-back murders always puts a little pep in Jessica's step." Jameson opened the email and skimmed through while Jameson and Dean waited patiently.

"Okay, so it confirms what we already know—the cause of death was multiple stab wounds. Unfortunately, she didn't find any evidence of the suspect's DNA. But wait a sec... she did find fibers under his finger nails."

"Fibers?"

"Polypropylene and nylon."

"Carpet fibers."

"He also had rug burns on his arms."

"So he was killed on a carpet, presumably, and tried to get away from his attacker."

Jonas cocked his head. "Wait, the bathroom where we found his body doesn't have carpet."

"That's right."

Dean sipped his coffee and said, "This confirms what we've already suspected. He wasn't killed in that bathroom. He was placed there, after the fact."

"To setup the kids who were staying in the room."

"Right."

"He had to have been killed somewhere close by, and what? The killer wrapped up his body in something and tossed him in the bathroom?"

Jameson scratched his head. "Let's have Hayes go through the trash cans again."

Dean nodded.

"We're missing something. Something in that house."

"Agreed."

❧

The early morning sun crept its way into the bedroom through a slit in the curtains. Jolene rolled over to see Ethan's sleepy eyes on her, and a smile spread across his lips.

"Good morning, beautiful."

Her heart skipped a beat and she smiled back. "Good morning."

He kissed her forehead. "How did you sleep?"

"Surprisingly well."

"Good."

"Coffee?"

"*Yes.*"

After the storm had cleared and Jolene was able to pull Ethan away from work, they'd picked up where they'd left off at her apartment, on the kitchen floor. And then, later, in the bedroom.

They'd laid in bed afterward and talked about nothing in particular, nothing heavy—which was exactly what she preferred—until they fell asleep.

She couldn't remember the last time she'd stayed the

night with a man. Or had sex three times in one day. Okay, that part had definitely never happened before.

She watched Ethan push out of bed and search the room for his boxer shorts that had been thrown off during their night of passion.

He was so handsome, so much more than when she'd first met him. Which only meant one thing—she was beginning to fall for him. Hard.

Her stomach tickled with nerves as the thought seemed to explode in her brain. She was falling for him, yes she was. Was he falling for her? Did he feel the same? How would it work? They lived very, *very* different lives, both driven by a very different code of ethics. She lived her life skirting around the very laws he'd taken an oath to protect.

She squeezed her eyes shut, trying to shake the thoughts from her head.

"You okay?" Ethan sat on the bed next to her and stroked her head.

"Yeah. Yes."

He looked at her for a long moment, then said, "I know things are complicated here." Pause. "Very complicated."

She nodded, the side of her face rubbing against the pillow.

A moment ticked by. "One thing my dad taught me was, when things get complicated, take it one thing at a time. Day by day. Hour by hour. And this hour, this minute, this second, I know there is nowhere in the world I'd rather be than sitting right here, looking at your beautiful face."

She melted, smiled.

"Let's just get some coffee, okay?"

She exhaled. "Okay."

Ten minutes later they sat at the breakfast table with two fresh cups of coffee, bagels warm from the toaster oven, and a spread of cream cheese, jelly and butter.

"So," he looked up from his bagel and narrowed his eyes, "I want you to stay here today."

She cocked an eyebrow. "Why?"

"Whoever sent you that letter obviously knows where you live. Until we figure out exactly who sent it and what they want, I'd like you to stay here. You're safer here."

"I'll find out who it is and what they want tonight at ten, at the cove."

He set down his coffee. "We already talked about this. I don't want you going to that meeting."

"Look, Ethan, I've taken care of myself my whole life. Tonight won't be any different. I'm not stupid, either. If I sense something, or if something seems off, I'll hightail it out of there."

He slowly sipped his coffee, watching her over the rim. "Alright. Then I go, too."

"You can't. They might get spooked."

"I'll stay back. Trust me; they won't even know I'm there."

She blew out a breath. "Fine."

He grinned; the satisfaction of winning written all over his face. "That's settled then. Okay, I've got a few errands to run this morning and then I'll be back." He drained his coffee, pushed back in his chair, and glanced over his shoulder before walking down the hall.

"Don't leave here today, Jolene."

CHAPTER 21

"GOOD MORNING, SUNSHINE." Ethan handed Jessica a cup of eight-dollar coffee—the good stuff. "Did you even leave last night?"

Her sleepy eyes lit up as her hand shot forward, grabbing the to-go cup. "Yeah, to shower."

He glanced past her into the lab. "Who do you have back there now?"

"Miss Debbie. I finished Chase's autopsy yesterday. I've got to get Debbie's done today."

"You really are swimming in dead bodies."

She paused, her eyes darkened. "Let's just hope I don't get any more today." A moment of silence weighed down the room. "Anyway, you got the envelope?"

He reached into his coat pocket, pulled out a plastic bag and handed it to her.

"Look's official. Where'd you get it?"

"It was sent to a friend of mine."

She turned it over in her hands.

"I'm hoping you can figure out who sent it."

"*If* I find any DNA, I'm not sure that I'll be able to get you a name, but I'll see what I can do."

"Thanks. And I need it as soon as possible, today."

She raised her eyebrows and held out her hand.

He laughed and grabbed his wallet. "I almost forgot. Two, right?"

"Four."

He shook his head. "Man, I'm in the wrong field."

She laughed as Ethan handed her four one-hundred dollar bills, and before he put his wallet back in his pocket, he pulled out a single dollar bill and handed it to her. "And this is for letting me see Debbie."

"A whole dollar?"

"Yep. Don't spend it all in one place."

She laughed and motioned him to follow her. "Come on back."

The cold air slapped him in the face as he stepped into the sterile, grey laboratory. The air carried a scent of chemicals and death.

"You got a weak stomach?"

"Only for brussel sprouts."

"Good."

Just ahead of him he saw Debbie's naked, grey body lying on a silver table. Her skin was split down the center of her torso, between the multiple stab wounds in her stomach.

"I was just about to dive inside."

Ethan looked down at her, remembering how she'd looked on their date, just hours before she'd been brutally murdered. She was beautiful, energetic. Alive. Her blonde hair had been perfectly curled, and now, it laid in a matted mess around her head. Who had taken her life? Who would do such a thing?

Was he the last person to see her alive? The thought sent a chill up his spine.

This wasn't the first dead body Ethan had seen; regardless, it always left him feeling restless, and oddly enough, reflective. To see the finality of death with his own eyes had a way of making him think of his own mortality. And of those he loved the most as well. It was a thought that always made him uneasy.

He looked her over, his gaze stopping on the lacerations. "How many stab wounds?"

"Seven. Four in the back, three in the abdomen."

He blew out a breath, "Seven," and shook his head. "One or two is an escalation of events, self-defense, or premeditated. Seven is a fit of rage, uncontrolled rage."

"My thoughts exactly. Most stabbings I see are, like you said, one or two stabs and then the killer snaps out of it, so to speak, and runs away or whatever." She shook her head. "Someone risked the extra time it took to keep stabbing. You're right; uncontrolled rage."

"Was it the same with Chase?"

Her eyes met his and a darkness of fear swept over her face. "Yes, exactly the same."

He was hoping she wasn't going to say that, but he wasn't surprised. His gut had been telling him the same thing.

She glanced down at the body. "It was a six-inch serrated blade that pierced both Chase's and Debbie's skin, *and* the stabbing locations are similar."

"Meaning, the killer knows where to hit for most impact."

She nodded. "It's not my job to determine if the same person murdered both Chase and Debbie, but in my opinion, there's too much of a coincidence—blade, stabbing locations, both were just a few days apart. Let me put it this way, I'd be shocked if they weren't killed by the same person." She sipped her coffee. "And as if these two murders weren't enough, you heard about the bones they pulled from Otter Lake, right?"

"Yeah, Jameson told me about it the day it happened. Have they made an ID?"

"Yep. Lisa Halstead, a senator's daughter."

He raised his eyebrows. "No shit?"

"No shit. She was kidnapped fifteen years ago. Held for ransom."

His stomach dropped to his feet. "Did you say ransom?"

"Yep."

His mind started racing. "Do you have the report?"

"No, but I can pull it." Ethan followed her as she crossed the room to her computer. After a few logins, she skimmed the state crime lab's database. "Ah, Lisa Halstead, here it is."

Ethan leaned forward as she pulled up the final report. "Bones estimated to be fifteen years old… environmental elements… submerged in water… blah, blah, blah…"

"Wait, stop." He pointed to the screen. "Scroll back up."

As she read the words under his finger, her mouth gaped open. "Tool marks noted on thoracic vertebra. Oh, my God."

"Her rib cage."

"Yes, and it says here that they've forwarded the bones to a forensic anthropologist for further analysis."

"That will take weeks."

Jessica turned, wide-eyed. "Do you think she was stabbed, too?"

"More often than not, tool marks mean a knife." He straightened. "I've got to go make some phone calls. Let me know what you find on that envelope as soon as possible."

"Will do."

"Thanks."

As Ethan pushed out the front doors, he reached for his phone.

"Miller here."

"Miller, hey it's Veech."

"Hey, how's vacation?"

He almost laughed. Vacation? What vacation? "It's been interesting to say the least."

"Yeah, how so?"

"Two dead bodies and missing senator's daughter found, fifteen years missing. Well, her bones at least."

"Whoa, whoa, where?"

"Here in Berry Springs."

"Arkansas?"

"Right."

"What the hell? What was the senator's daughter's name?"

"Lisa Halstead."

"Hmm, doesn't ring a bell. I'll look it up."

"Yeah, can you send me the notes on the case?"

"You got it. What about the other bodies? Murders?"

"Yep, stabbings."

"Well, shit, man. Sounds crazy down there. You involved?"

He thought of his date with Debbie, and of his relationship with Jolene, who was the last person to see Chase

Martinez alive. "You could say that. Hey, I've got some code I'm going to send you."

"Code?"

"Yeah, I think it's a ransomware virus, but it's different than what I've seen. Need another set of eyes on it."

"You've come to the right place. No problem at all. Where'd you get it?"

He hesitated. "You asked me to dig deeper into Packer, right? Off the grid."

"Yeah…"

"This is part of it."

"Care to give me more details?"

His gut was screaming at him that there was a connection between the ransom for the senator's daughter fifteen years ago; the two murders; and Bia's ransomware virus, but he had nothing concrete to base the assumption on. And the bureau was only interested in facts, not gut instincts. "Not yet, brother."

"Understood."

"Send me the info on Lisa Halstead, and I'll shoot you the code today for you to look over."

"Will do, and sounds good."

"Talk soon."

"Ethan?"

"Yeah?"

"Be smart."

"Always."

Click.

He jumped into his truck just as his cell phone rang.

"Veech."

"Veech, hey, it's Jameson."

"Hey, how's it going?"

"Haven't slept in two days."

"Any developments on Chase or Debbie?"

He heard an exhausted sigh through the phone. "Not nearly as much as I'd like, which is why I'm calling you."

"Anything you need."

"Thanks. We're going back through Chase's murder with a fine-toothed comb. We've re-interviewed the couple that was staying in the room…"

"Mark Williams and Tiffany Lancaster."

"Right. And we're taking another look through the B&B, the trash cans, etcetera. Anyway, Jonas has been looking into the girl living upstairs. Anna Gable, I believe."

Ethan's stomach dropped.

"We couldn't find anything on her, anywhere. So we checked in the DMV database and I'll be damned, we can't find anyone with that name, within her age range, or height. Anywhere."

Ethan's pulse picked up as he desperately tried to think of something to say, or buy some time, at least. "Are you sure? Maybe he should try to run it again?"

"He did. Ran it twice. Nothing. So Dean dropped by her place first thing this morning, but she wasn't there."

Shit.

"And this brings me to you. Any way you can run her in the FBI database or something?"

"Of course, no problem. Hey, did you try Anne, or maybe Anna is short for something, like Anastasia." Damn, he was reaching.

"Tried everything we can think of, but I gotta tell ya, my radar is going off like crazy. Unless you can find her, then I'm assuming she gave us a fake name. Considering that, and the fact that she lives upstairs, *and* was the one to find Chase's body, we've got more than enough reason to bring her in."

Shit, shit, shit, shit.

"Yep, no problem man, will run her as soon as I can."

"Today?"

Pause. "Will do, buddy."

"Thanks."

CHAPTER 22

*D*ON'T LEAVE HERE *today.*

That was the last thing Ethan had said to her before walking out. To say that it rubbed her wrong was an understatement, and more than that, she'd never been one to take orders from anyone. Especially a man. Especially a man that she had somewhat of a relationship… no, a *situation*, with.

They weren't in a relationship. Not even close. And even though he gave her butterflies, turned her head to mush, and hell, seemed to take over her body, they lived totally different lives. She knew it, and she knew that he knew it. It was written all over his face this morning.

What the hell was she thinking?

She *wasn't* thinking. She was letting her emotions get the best of her.

Feeling antsy and agitated, she walked out of the back door and stepped onto the porch. It was a dreary, cool, fall morning. Thick cloud cover blocked the sun, and in the west, dark clouds loomed.

Another storm coming in.

A cool breeze swept up her back and she wrapped her arms around herself.

She sat on the porch swing and decided to address the thoughts that had been swirling in her head since she'd made the deal with Ethan.

Was it time to turn her life around? Climb her way out of the dark hole she'd dug for herself and start over? Maybe get a traditional job, a home, and maybe even a dog. Definitely not a cat—she'd never been a cat person.

The deal she made with Ethan could be the start. She'd have her slate wiped clean and could lay low for a bit while she devised a plan to close the door on her past.

But what about the job Dylan had lined up for her? It was a lot of money. A *hell* of a lot of money.

She took a deep breath and gazed up at the sky. A crow called out from the top of a leafless tree, then took flight, its black wings fitting perfectly against the grey, omi- nous clouds.

One thing she was certain of was that it was time to leave the little, country town of Berry Springs, Arkansas. As soon as she completed her end of the deal with Ethan, she'd be gone. And she'd figure out the rest of her life later.

Don't leave here today.

She rolled her eyes, shook her head, and pushed off the swing. He wasn't her boss, and regardless of what happened between them, he never would be.

She contemplated.

Well, she needed a change of clothes, didn't she? And, today she could tell Barb that she'd be gone by the end of the week. Lastly, but perhaps most importantly, she wanted to know if Barb had seen anyone lurking around the house with an envelope in their hand the night before.

Yep, she had things to do.

Two hours later, Jolene rolled to a stop in front of the B&B, turned off the engine, and got out of the car. Twigs and leaves scattered the yard from the storm the night before, and a large limb lay across the sidewalk.

As she stepped onto the walkway, something moved in the corner of her eye.

"Anna?"

She turned to see old Mrs. Chapman, shuffling across the lawn in a terry cloth pink bathrobe and slippers.

"Hi, Mrs. Chapman. How are you today?"

"I'm good, dear," she reached out her hand which was almost as shaky as her voice. "What an awful couple of days it's been, hasn't it?"

The woman didn't know the half of it. "It sure has."

Mrs. Chapman lowered her voice and leaned forward. "I heard the man who died was stabbed to death. Is that true?"

Jolene glanced down for a moment, then nodded.

"Oh, how terrible, dear. Were you home when it happened?"

"No, I wasn't."

"Do the cops have any suspects?"

"I'm really not sure."

"I heard something, you know."

"Heard something?"

Mrs. Chapman whispered, "Screams. His screams."

"Are you sure?"

Mrs. Chapman nodded and shook her head. "And now, that poor girl who worked at the diner. What was her name again?"

"Debbie, I think."

"Yes, that's right. She was stabbed, too, right? In the park."

Why was Mrs. Chapman asking her all these questions?

She continued, "That's what I heard, hon. It doesn't take a rocket scientist to figure out that it must've been the same person who did it."

The back of Jolene's neck prickled and she looked around the yard. Looking for what, she wasn't sure, but something made her feel like they weren't alone.

"I just can't believe the cops haven't arrested anyone yet. I saw them poking around here again today."

"You did?"

"Yeah, that good looking one, what's his name…" she squeezed her eyes shut. "Officer… Dean. Officer Dean. Boy, he's a dandy, isn't he? Anyway, he came by here this morning and there's been a few others walking the area again today."

She broke into a sweat. Why would the police come by a second time? She glanced at the house, then back to Mrs. Chapman. "I need to get going." *Literally.*

"Okay, dear."

She turned and began walking across the yard.

"Anna?"

She stopped, looked over her shoulder.

A dark cloud shaded Mrs. Chapman's face as she said, "Watch yourself."

The cool wind whipped dead leaves around her ankles.

"Yes, ma'am." Feeling uneasy, she turned and walked up the porch steps and into the house.

The house was quiet, still. She heard low conversation in the kitchen as she closed the door behind her.

"Barb?" She walked down the hall.

"Hi, dear." With her hands wrapped around a warm cup of tea, Barb looked up from the kitchen table.

"I see the electricity's back on." Jolene glanced over at the sink, where Greg busied himself with dishes. "Hey, Greg."

"Hey. How's it going?" He looked different—stressed. His eyes were sunken in and shaded with dark circles. His face, which was already pale, was whiter than a ghost.

The air was heavy in the room, weighed by something Jolene couldn't quite put her finger on. She looked from Barb, to Greg, then back at Barb. "Everything okay?"

"Oh, yes," Barb shook her head as if to shake away the bad energy. "Just sick of all this." She glanced at Greg. "Poor Debbie. This is all just too much."

Jolene dropped her purse on the table and sank into the chair across from Barb. "I know it's awful."

"Want some tea?"

"No, thanks, Greg. I didn't expect to see you here today."

"Just checkin' on Barb. Hell of a storm last night." He looked down. "Hell of a freakin' night."

Jolene looked at him. What the hell was going on?

Barb glanced at Greg, and then back and Jolene and nodded. "It sure was. Did you see that limb in the front yard? It was lying across the driveway until Greg moved it."

"Yeah, I saw it." A moment ticked by. "I heard the cops came back today."

Greg shuttered.

"Where'd you hear that?"

"Mrs. Chapman."

"The gossip, of course."

"So they did?"

"Yes, took another look around and asked about you, actually."

Greg glanced over, suddenly listening intently.

Barb continued, "They wanted to speak with you again, and when I told them you weren't here, they asked if I knew where you'd gone."

Jolene's pulse picked up. Had they figured out the connection between her and Chase? Did they know her real name wasn't Anna? She bit the inside of her cheek, trying to mask her emotions even though her heart was pounding.

"Did they say what they wanted?"

"Probably just a formality," Greg said.

She shifted in her seat, her stomach churning. "Yeah, you're probably right."

Barb sipped her tea. "So where were you last night?"

"At a friend's."

Barb grinned. "A *male* friend?"

Jolene rolled her eyes. "Yes, a male friend, and no, I'm not answering any more questions." She paused. "To you, or the damn cops."

"Okay, dear, and I wouldn't worry about them."

She took a deep breath. "Anything else? Are they any closer to finding the murderer?"

Barb sighed. "Not that I'm aware of. They were here forever, though. I even saw that young cop poking through the trash can. I think they even walked down to the lake."

"Find anything?"

Barb scoffed. "Like they would tell me."

She made a mental note to ask Ethan as soon as she saw him.

"Is anything else going on with you, dear?"

"I actually do have something to ask you. Did you happen to see anyone in the house last night?"

"Last night? Well, it was as black as a bat's wing in this place."

"I mean before the electricity went out. Maybe late afternoon or early evening."

Barb closed her eyes, searching her memory. "I don't think so. I'm sure I had the doors locked." She opened her eyes and looked at Jolene. "Why?"

"Just curious." She stood grabbed her purse. "One more thing, I wanted to let you know that I plan to be out by the end of the week."

Barb set down her tea. "Really? I hate to hear that, dear. You've been a wonderful tenant."

Jolene smiled. "Thank you. It's just time for me to move on."

Barb stared at her for a moment and then smiled. "Understood, dear."

Jolene glanced at Greg. "Have a good one, Greg."

"I'm actually about to head out, too." He looked at Barb. "Any idea when we'll be back in business?"

"Maybe next week. I wanted to wait until after they made an arrest, but who knows when that will be."

Greg looked down for a moment before saying, "Alright, ladies, have a good afternoon."

"You, too."

Jolene walked up the creaky, wooden staircase to her apartment and paused on the second floor. Although it had been days since the murder, the faint smell of chemicals still hung in the air. She walked to the room where Chase had been murdered and leaned against the doorframe. Their last conversation replayed in her head—an argument over money.

Damn money.

Goosebumps ran over her arms as the image of Chase's stabbed, mutilated body flashed in her head.

She wrapped her arms around herself.

Silence buzzed in her ears.

A chill ran like fingertips up her spine.

Creak.

Her heart stopped. She turned.

WHACK!

CHAPTER 23

PAIN SHOT THROUGH her body as she blinked open her eyes. The blurriness sent a wave of nausea through her stomach.

BAM!

Her head bounced off of something.

BAM!

Again.

She squinted and looked around, trying to make sense of what was happening.

Something covered her mouth—duct tape—her hands and ankles were bound, and she was being dragged down the staircase by her feet.

By Barb.

Barb.

"Waking up, huh?"

She inhaled and tried to scream through the duct tape.

Winded, Barb said, "Go ahead and make all the noise you want, no one's here to help you."

Her head bounced down another step.

"*Phew*, it's exhausting dragging you down here, but

a hell of a lot better than dragging a body upstairs, that's for sure."

Her head bounced down what seemed like a hundred more steps before her body hit the first floor like dead weight. She frantically looked up at the front windows, praying that someone would walk up. It was darker outside. How long had she been out? The last thing she remembered seeing was Barb swinging a baseball bat at her head.

Barb—she couldn't believe it. Her mind raced, what the hell was going on?

"Just one more flight."

One more flight? Barb was taking her to the basement, where she lived.

She thought of Ethan. Would he realize she'd left and come looking for her? Would he think to check in the basement? Of course not.

Shit.

Barb took a moment to catch her breath and then bent down, picked up Jolene's feet and began dragging her down the hall. Strands of her hair caught on the hardwood planks, ripping each from her head.

Confusion was replaced with panic. She had to get the hell out of there. Somehow.

Where was Greg? Had he left already?

Barb unlocked the door that led down to the basement, took a deep breath, and pulled Jolene's body down the final set of stairs.

With a hard *thud*, she was left at the bottom of the staircase, with full view of the space.

Although it was technically the basement, it didn't look like one. It looked like an upscale, newly-renovated apartment with top-of-the-line appliances and furniture. Hell, it looked like a multi-million dollar New York apartment.

Marble floors ran across a large living room with bright white sofas that sat in front of a big screen television. Expensive paintings lined the walls. Lush plants and house trees were placed throughout, and unlit candles decorated the surfaces. The kitchen, in grey and white marble, sat off to the side. A hallway, with lush carpet, decorated with authentic oriental rugs, ran to the left and right, presumably to more rooms.

Barb had some money. More than anyone would've guessed.

It was perfectly tidy, too, without a speck of dust anywhere. Everything had a place, in perfect ninety-degree angles. Every color and fabric strategically placed.

"I'll be right back. Don't go anywhere." Barb chuckled as she walked down the hall.

Jolene began frantically trying to loosen her bindings, while her eyes searched for an escape.

As she bucked, her body shifted and her gaze landed on a desk in the far side of the living room. Multiple computer monitors and screens lined the wall. It looked like a command center that one would find in the FBI building or something.

What the hell?

She scanned the screens and—*wait*—was that Ethan's kitchen? Her stomach dropped. The kitchen table where they had just had breakfast hours earlier was displayed on the center monitor. His computer set on the kitchen table in the background.

Why the hell was Barb spying on Ethan?

&

Ethan drove up the steep driveway to the cabin. Bright beams of late afternoon sun shot out from the thick cloud cover, looking like gold spears from the sky.

As he parked, his instincts piqued. Something wasn't right; he could feel it.

He got out of his truck, walked up the porch steps and before he'd even opened the door, he knew.

She'd left. Exactly like he'd told her not to.

He stepped inside. The air was still, the house was vacant.

Dammit.

Why the hell did this woman have such a hard time listening to him? Maybe because he'd *told* her not to go anywhere instead of *asking* her. But what the hell? He was looking out for her safety and now was not the time to go all feminist on him. Although, as much as he hated to admit it, her independence was one of the things that attracted him to her most. Damn it, why couldn't he fall in love with a normal, sweet girl with zero baggage?

Because she'd bore the hell out of him, that's why.

He walked through the house, pausing in the bedroom. The scent of her skin lingered in the air. The bedspread lay crumpled on the floor, the sheets strewn across the bed, where they had made love not eight hours earlier.

God, she was beautiful. Every inch of her mesmerized him. Her hair, her body, those eyes. Those deep brown eyes that could cut right through him.

Taking a deep breath, he turned and walked into the kitchen. A note lay on the table.

Be back later. Don't worry.

He picked it up and crumpled it in his hand. No, she sure as hell didn't listen to him.

He pulled his cell phone from his pocket and dialed her number.

Voicemail. Dammit.

He slid it back into his pocket and glanced at the clock — just after six. Four hours before her meeting at the cove.

Something in his gut twisted. He didn't feel quite right. Why?

Antsy now, he grabbed a beer, his laptop, and sat at the table. Maybe Miller had forwarded the information on Lisa Halstead.

He powered it up and opened his email. Yep, there it was. Miller had sent him the Halstead file.

He quickly sent Miller the code he'd pulled from Bia's computer and then settled in to read about Lisa.

Her file was as thick as he'd expected.

Lisa was only seventeen when she was kidnapped. An only child to a wealthy family, rich in both money and legacy, Lisa grew up in a sheltered society full of toys and whatever else she wanted. Her father, Kevin Halstead, was elected into the US Senate at the age of forty-three, shortly after his father retired his seat. Three weeks after Lisa's seventeenth birthday, she went out for a jog and was never seen or heard from again. The case was quickly forwarded to the FBI, and forty-eight hours after she'd been officially declared a missing person, a note was hand-delivered to the Halstead home, demanding two million dollars ransom for their only daughter. The Halstead home had tight security which included outdoor cameras; however, as luck would have it, two of those cameras were out. One did catch a glimpse of the suspect on the front lawn, wearing head-to-toe black and a baseball cap. Five-eleven, a one-hundred and thirty-pound Hispanic male.

Perhaps due to the flurry of media attention, the deadline for the cash was moved up, and when the demand wasn't met, that was the end of Lisa Halstead's life. Was she drowned? Or stabbed to death as the tool marks on her bones indicate?

Ethan grabbed his beer and took a deep sip.

A hand-delivered note.

Ransom.

Stabbing.

Coincidence? No way in hell.

Almost two hours—and three more unanswered calls to Jolene's cell phone—had passed since he'd come home to an empty house. Where the hell was she?

He pushed out of the chair and began pacing. Darkness had fallen.

He walked to the window and gazed out. Less than two hours to the arranged meeting at the cove.

Dammit, Jolene, where are you?

He picked up the note she'd left him and read it again.

Be back later. Don't worry.

Don't worry. Yeah, right.

He grabbed his cell phone and dialed her number, again.

Sorry you missed me, please leave…

He clicked off and couldn't ignore the pit in his stomach. Something was wrong. He dialed one more time. No answer.

He made another call.

Hi, you've reached Jessica Heathrow, Medical Examiner, I'm away from my phone right now. Please leave a message and I'll get back to you.

"Jessica, hey, it's Ethan. Just checking on the DNA results from the envelope. Give me a call as soon as you can."

He tried Jolene one more time before tossing the phone on the counter.

Fuck this.

As he reached for his car keys, his phone rang.

"Veech here."

"Hey, it's Jessica. Sorry it took me so long to get this done. Been crazy around here. I've got the results you asked for."

His pulse picked up. "Yeah?"

"I was able to pull some pretty solid DNA off the glue. It was licked." He heard paper rustling in the background. "Let's see, the person who licked the envelope… Age range fifty to sixty, Caucasian, female."

"*Female?*"

"Yep. You want more than that; you'll have to send it down state."

"You get a name?"

"Nope."

His head began spinning. "You're sure female?"

"One-hundred percent."

"Thanks, Jess."

"No problem. I'll leave it here for you to pick up whenever."

"Thanks."

Click.

He slid the phone into his pocket and stood frozen, processing the information.

White female, mid-fifties.

He began pacing the room, his heart racing.

White female, mid-fifties. Come on, Ethan.

He repeated the words over and over in his head until it hit him like lightning.

He grabbed his car keys from the kitchen table and as he spun around, they tumbled out of his hands and flung into the cabinet. As he reached forward, pictures tumbled to the ground and a red, blinking light caught his eye.

He froze, his eyes widened.

At his feet lay a small recorder.

"*Son of a bitch.*"

He turned it off, grabbed his keys, and bolted out of the door.

The black night closed in on him as he jumped into his truck and skidded out of the driveway. Barreling down the hill, he picked up his phone. No reception.

"*Dammit!*" He tossed it in his cup holder and pressed the gas.

Jolene craned her neck as she heard footsteps coming from down the hall. Carrying a rope and tarp, and the sheath of a knife secured to her belt, Barb stopped next to Jolene.

"I'd planned to meet you at ten o'clock but your little boyfriend changed those plans."

Jolene's eyes widened as the pieces of the puzzle began falling into place—ten o'clock, the envelope, the meeting at the cove, S.P.

Barb was Slade Packer.

Panic shot through her. She had to tell Ethan. How?

Barb knelt down and leaned in close to Jolene's face. "Jolene."

Her eyes widened. Barb knew her real name.

"That's right; I've known who you were since the moment I laid eyes on you. It's a small world in our line of work. Funny how you and I both ended up in little ol' Berry Springs. Anyway, we have an issue." Barb paused, choosing her words carefully, then said, "Mr. Veech has been getting a little too close to me lately, which I wouldn't have cared too much about, but he changed the game when he hacked into my friend Bia's computer and copied a piece of code we've been working very hard on. So Jolene, as you can see, I need that thumb drive." She leaned even closer. "Do you understand?"

Heart pounding, Jolene nodded.

"Good. I have to make a quick call."

Jolene strained to listen as Barb dialed from the kitchen.

"Mr. White, please... Allen, its Barb. Please get my plane ready immediately... I know it's short notice... in under an hour... yes, thank you, see you then."

Adrenaline rushed through her veins. Whatever Barb—Slade Packer—was going to do within the next hour; she was going to run afterward. Dammit, she had to tell Ethan!

"Where's your phone?"

Jolene tried to open her mouth, but her skin ripped against the duct tape.

"No, don't try to talk… do you have it with you now?"
She nodded and glanced down toward her pocket.

"Perfect." Barb reached into Jolene's back pocket and pulled out her cell phone.

As Barb typed a text message, Jolene glanced around, looking for any possible weapon or escape route.

"Smile." She glanced up just as Barb snapped her picture. "Alright, that should do it." Barb slid the phone into her pocket and looked at Jolene, her eyes cold as ice. "Let's get down to the lake."

CHAPTER 24

E THAN SKIDDED ONTO the highway and glanced down at his phone. Two bars. He picked it up and dialed.

"Jameson here."

"Jameson, its Veech. I need you to get to Barb's B&B immediately."

"What's going on? You okay?"

"Too much to explain. I'm about fifteen minutes away now; I need you to get there as soon as possible. Look for Barb, don't let her leave."

"Barb? You're joking. What…?"

Ethan hung up.

One new message.

He clicked it open and his heart sank. A spike of panic burst through his body as he stared down at the picture of Jolene, tied at the ankles and wrists, with silver duct tape covering her mouth.

Deliver the thumb drive to 418 Lake View Drive. Drop

in mailbox. If you call the cops, she dies. You have forty-five minutes.

He glanced at the clock—nine o'clock—and back down at his phone. The text was sent thirty minutes ago.

"*Fuck!*" He slammed his fist against the steering wheel and pressed the gas.

His heart hammered as the truck skidded around the hairpin turns of the Ozark Mountains. He glanced up at the sky as a cloud drifted across the moon.

By his estimate, he should arrive at the B&B at 9:15 exactly. Would he be too late?

❧

She took a deep breath as a black hood was placed over her head and darkness cloaked her. Her mouth was taped shut, hands and feet bound, and now, her vision stolen. Tears welled in her eyes as she was rolled onto the tarp.

Knock, knock, knock.

Barb dropped her feet and under her breath said, "What the hell?"

Knock, knock, knock.

After a moment, Barb's footsteps disappeared up the staircase. The door creaked open.

"*Well, hey, Greg, what can I do for ya?*"

"*Hey Barb, I left my damn jacket again. Do you know where it is?*"

A casual chuckle. "*You and that damn jacket. No, I don't. Check in the kitchen again?*"

A moment ticked by.

"*Found it, slid off the chair and under the table.*"

"Alright, you have a good night, dear. Try to relax. Lock the door on your way out."

"Alright. Night."

The door shut, then creaked opened again. Jolene had no doubt Barb was making sure he was gone before coming back downstairs.

Then, footsteps down the stairs.

"Well, that was close."

After a moment of shuffling, Jolene was slowly dragged onto the rock path that led down to the lake.

Each rock that her body slid over was like knives cutting into her back.

Would Ethan think to look for her at the lake? Would he come for her?

The tears in her eyes began to spill down her cheeks as hopelessness began to take hold. She felt the sting of a rock cut her back, followed by the warmth of blood.

This can't be happening.

The smell of lake water drifted through the air, followed by the sound of water lapping against the shoreline.

She was pulled onto the dock and dropped.

A squeaky door opened, then shut. Footsteps back and forth, back and forth.

Finally, the footsteps stopped next to her, and she was rolled into a boat.

Terror gripped her as she thought of the human bones that were recently pulled from the lake.

Were hers next?

Ethan. Save me, Ethan.

Suddenly, everything stopped. The only movement was the slow rocking of the boat, the only sound were the waves.

"Three more minutes."

Jolene twisted her neck toward Barb's voice and through the black fabric she saw the light of a cell phone in Barb's hand.

Her heart felt like it was going to explode.

"Two more minutes." Barb sighed and then said, "You thought I didn't know a thing about cameras or security. You couldn't have been more wrong, dear. Your boyfriend has about a minute and a half to drop the thumb drive in the mailbox, which I'm watching from one of my cameras." Pause. "Now a minute."

Jolene's stomach churned as the seconds ticked away.

"Time's up."

∽

Ethan skidded to a stop in front of the B&B and glanced at the clock before jumping out of the truck—9:18. He was three minutes late. His heart hammered as he shoved the thumb drive in the mailbox and sprinted up the walkway. He leapt onto the porch, tried the door. Locked.

"Jolene!"

He glanced in the front window before picking up a small outdoor table, turning it upside down, and ramming the iron legs through the glass. He popped the shattered pieces out and jumped through.

"*Jolene!*"

The house was dark and silent. A chill ran up his spine.

He bolted up the stairs, taking the steps three at a time until he reached the third floor. He tried Jolene's doorknob—unlocked—and burst through the door.

"Jolene!"

The room looked exactly as they had left it the night before, with his beer sitting on the coffee table, next to hers. He searched the bedroom, bathroom, closet.

Nothing.

He ran back down the stairs to the first floor, down the hall and to the door he'd assumed led to Barb's apartment.

Locked.

He reared back, slammed the full weight of his body into it, and almost tumbled down the staircase as the door burst open.

He flew down the steps and froze when he saw the command center. Each screen showed various angles of the B&B, as well as each floor. And the center screen was the recording of Ethan's kitchen, frozen on the last picture before he'd turned off the camera.

"Son of a bitch."

He jogged through the empty apartment. Where the hell was she?

He paused in the hallway and his gaze landed on the sliding glass door that led outside. It was pitch-black outside, but the light spilling from the kitchen illuminated the backyard. Bright fall leaves scattered the porch, except for a line leading to the trail. Something had been dragged across the porch. He jogged outside, his gut telling him he was onto something. Just past the porch, the gravel covering the manicured trail that led down to the lake was scattered, leaving the exposed dirt.

Something was dragged across the porch, and down to the lake.

He took off down the dark trail, barely able to see more

than a few feet in front of him. His chest heaved; his feet slid along the loose gravel every few feet.

He burst through the tree line and leapt onto the dock. "Jolene!"

The faint smell of gasoline hung in the air. He jogged to the edge of the dock, looked out to the lake and noticed two twinkling lights in the distance.

His heart skipped madly in his chest. The main boat slip was empty, but a small fishing boat was tied on the far side.

He jumped in and frantically searched for the keys.

"*Come on, come on.*"

His fingertips searched under the seat, and *Bingo*!

The boat sputtered to life and he took off into the dark night. He clicked off all the lights and steered toward the boat in the distance, with not a doubt in his mind that he would find Jolene there. But would he be too late?

CHAPTER 25

TIME'S UP.

Her chest seized with panic as the boat sped through the dark night. The cool evening air whipped around her body as she lay gagged, tied and hooded on the floor.

Ethan was not coming.

No one was going to save her.

Tears flowed down her face, and after what seemed like just a few minutes, the boat finally slowed and stopped.

Her heart sank.

She heard Barb's footsteps around her and then a *thud* of something heavy. As Barb began to tie something to her feet, she said, "You know, Jolene, I actually hate to do this. I admire your work; I really do. I've had my eye on you for years. It's a shame. I think you would've been an asset to my team."

She began to sob as Barb pulled her up. "But unfortunately, your boyfriend screwed that up for you and, as you can see, I guess he didn't care too much about you."

Her breath stopped as she was hoisted into the air.

Her head lobbed over the side of the boat as Barb worked to inch her over the side.

"Dammit, some help would be nice."

Cold lake water saturated the top of her head as her shoulders inched over.

"*Stop!*"

Jolene's eyes shot open just before her body slid into the water, followed by the splash of the cinder block that was tied to her feet.

꩜

Ethan rammed his boat into the side of Barb's boat and dove into the churning water. He opened his eyes to total darkness.

Oh, God, where is she?

He swam further down, his legs kicking wildly, his hope fading with each inch, until, he felt her.

His hand gripped her arm, yanking her forward. But as hard as he fought, they were being dragged down, together.

Adrenaline burst through his veins as he dove deeper, grabbed her feet and slid off the rope. She kicked frantically as he grabbed her arm, pulling her higher, and higher, until her head burst through the water. As she gasped and sputtered, he ripped the hood off of her.

"My hands." She coughed. "My hands."

He dove under and ripped the band from her wrists.

"Are you okay?"

In between breaths she nodded. "Yes."

"Hang onto me." He looked around and saw Barb speeding off in the distance. His jaw clenched. He'd get her.

He pulled Jolene into the small fishing boat, knelt down and wrapped his arms around her shivering body.

Chest heaving, she collapsed into his arms and gripped him almost as hard as he gripped her.

He closed his eyes and stroked her head. "You're okay. Everything's okay."

She nestled closer, closed her eyes, and wept.

∾

Jameson turned off the engine and looked at the B&B, his eyes landing on the busted window.

"Dammit."

As he got out, another squad car pulled behind him.

"Hey."

"Hey, Dean."

They met on the front lawn.

"What's going on?"

Jameson glanced at his phone. "Ethan called me, sounded panicked, and told me to get here as soon as I could. Said not to let Barb leave."

Dean drew his gun as he looked at the window. "*Barb*? He say why?"

"Nope."

"I'll go around back, you stay up front."

"You got it."

Jameson pulled his gun and walked onto the porch. Window busted out; front door locked. Not good. He edged himself through the window, raised his gun and stepped inside.

"Barb?"

Nothing.

After scanning the room, he walked down the hall where the door to Barb's apartment stood open.

Following his gut, he slowly descended the staircase. At the bottom of the stairs, his gaze landed on the command center.

"What the fuck?"

He walked over, looking at each screen. Most were streaming videos of the B&B and the grounds, but some were of other places entirely. His mouth dropped as he recognized one of the rooms—Chief McCord's office—and another screen ran the transcripts of each call sent to dispatch. She'd been keeping tabs on them.

What the hell was she up to?

He shook his head and looked around. The apartment was immaculate. As clean as a damn hospital room and everything had its place… except for a random rug lying haphazardly in the hall. He walked over and bent down.

Dean walked through the sliding glass doors. "No one's outside. Her red truck is in the garage. What'd you find?"

Jameson pulled away the rug and the faint smell of bleach floated up.

"Smells interesting."

"Sure does." He ran his finger along the side of the trim and lifted up the carpet. "It's been cut away."

Dean knelt down. "Uh-oh, Barb."

Faded red stains covered the concrete.

"You got your light?"

"Yep." Dean stood, turned off the lights, bent back down, and flicked on his fluorescent light.

"Holy shit."

The UV light illuminated hundreds of blood spatters on the wall and a puddle on the concrete floor underneath. Jameson shook his head and looked at Dean. "How much you wanna bet this blood belongs to Chase Martinez?"

"Killed him down here, dragged him upstairs to frame the guests. Yep, makes sense to me." Dean pushed off the floor. "Where the hell is she?" He looked around, then turned on his heel. "I'm going down to the lake; you calling the team?"

"Yep."

∽

Ethan hugged her tighter, in tune to every inhale, exhale, every tear that dropped from her face.

He'd almost lost her. A minute later and she would have been gone forever. The thought churned his stomach… and pissed him the hell off. Real bad. Anger started to bubble up as he thought of what he was going to do when he caught up with Barb, aka Slade Packer. He had to get Jameson, Dean, or someone to go after her. Immediately.

He gripped Jolene tighter, kissed the top of her head and whispered in her ear, "You're okay now. Everything's going to be okay."

A cloud drifted from the moon allowing the silver light to spill over the boat. He lifted his arm to stroke her hair and noticed spots of red on his shirt.

"Jolene, are you bleeding? You're bleeding."

She opened her eyes and looked up. "What?"

He pulled away, panic washing over his face. "Where… are you hurt? Where is the blood coming from?"

His heart began to race as he looked her over. Was she stabbed like all the others?

Oh, God, please no.

He lifted the back of her shirt. Streaks of red ran the entire length of her back, where welts and purple bruises were beginning to form.

"Oh, my God, baby."

Her teeth chattered. "She dragged me down the hill."

Ethan clenched his jaw, rage filling his veins.

Not now, need a clear head now.

He looked toward the shore and then back at Jolene. "Okay, we've got to get back." He pulled away and gripped her shoulders. "You're going to be okay, I've got to get you to the hospital." He eased her down to the floor of the boat and covered her with his shirt. "Just a few minutes and we'll be back. I'm right here." After kissing her forehead he started the engine, turned the boat around, and gunned it back to the shore.

As the dock came into view, he saw the outline of a man looking out to the lake.

Dean.

He drifted to the dock and Dean pulled him in, securing the boat to the side. Dean took one glance at Jolene and grabbed his radio.

"Get a medic here immediately." He jumped in the boat. "She okay? You okay?"

Ethan carefully picked her up off the floor. "She needs to get to the hospital." He stepped out of the boat and onto the dock, with Dean on his heels. "Barb's real name is Slade Packer, she just tried to kill Jolene and I have a feeling she's also responsible for Chase's and Debbie's deaths."

With Jolene cradled in his arms, they walked briskly up the trail.

Dean lit the way with his flashlight. "We found blood spatters in Barb's apartment, covered up. Definitely could be Chase's. What makes you think she murdered Debbie too?"

"Because she was trying to get to me. Possibly send me a message. I've been tracking her for weeks. She's responsible for hacking into the Pentagon, and now, developing a ransomware virus to hold our nukes hostage."

"How do you know?"

"Too much to get into now, but, hostages, ransom; that's her thing."

"And stabbings."

Ethan nodded. "The senator's daughter—the bones you just found—Lisa was stabbed. Talk to Jessica Heathrow. The girl was stabbed and held for ransom, and then thrown in Otter Lake. Seems like quite the coincidence."

"I don't believe in coincidences."

"Neither do I." They stepped off the trail and onto the lawn as the wailing of sirens screamed through the air.

"Barb took off, northwest I believe, in her boat."

"She's rich right?"

"Millionaire. Living here was a ruse—fake name, fake persona. I'm sure she has mansions all over the world that she visits."

Dean nodded. "I'm assuming she's got her own plane then, and northwest would take her to the airport." Dean looked at Ethan. "You take care of her. I'll get Packer."

Dean took off in a jog as Jameson walked up. "Holy shit, y'all okay?"

"Ambulance here?"

"Just pulled up."

They fell into step together.

"Call Dean, or better yet, you might want to go with him right now."

"What? Where?"

"To arrest Barb; real name Slade Packer."

"Slade Packer? The dude who hacked into the Pentagon?"

"A woman, and yes."

Jameson glanced up the hill where Dean was jumping into his squad car. He looked back at Ethan, then down at Jolene. "You sure she's okay?"

"Yes, go."

"*Dean, wait!*" Jameson took off up the hill.

The house was swarming with police as Ethan carried Jolene to the ambulance. The medics jumped out of the back and took Jolene from his arms.

"What's her name?"

"Jolene Reeves."

"What happened?"

"She was dragged downhill on her back, and then," his voice cracked, surprising him with emotion, "attempted murder by drowning."

"Okay, sir, we'll take it from here."

"No, you won't." Ethan jumped in the back. "I'm going with you."

CHAPTER 26

ASHIVER RAN UP his spine as he paced outside of the hospital room. God, he hated hospitals.

The door opened and he spun on his heel.

"Not just yet, sir." The nurse said.

He blew out a breath and glanced at the clock. Two in the morning.

Jolene was worse than he'd thought. Not only was her back sliced to shreds and internal organs bruised, but she had a pulmonary edema—fluid in the lungs—from almost drowning. She had been in intensive care with restricted access for the last four hours.

He'd received several calls and texts from Jameson as the evening had progressed. Apparently, Jameson and Dean arrived at the airport just as Packer was boarding her private jet. She was arrested on the spot and taken to the city jail where she was waiting patiently for her team of high profile lawyers to show up.

Would be a hell of a case, no doubt about that.

Ethan had emailed Miller and asked him for the DNA results of the envelope that was left for Lisa Halstead's dad, fifteen years ago. He had no doubt in his mind that it was licked by a woman as well. By Slade Packer herself.

He paused at the end of the hall, and blankly stared out the window into the dark night.

He'd almost lost her. He almost lost Jolene and the thought completely jarred him. Not just because a life was almost lost, but because he'd come to realize that he was head over heels in love with her. That he couldn't imagine spending a day without her.

His stomach clenched with emotion.

"Mr. Veech?"

Ethan turned. "Yes?"

"You can see her now."

He jogged down the hall and stepped into Jolene's room. His heart leapt out of his chest as she smiled a sleepy smile when she saw him.

She had an oxygen line on her nose, and an IV drip in each arm. He walked to the side of her bed and lightly grabbed her hand.

"Hi." He smiled

"Hi. You stayed."

"Of course."

"Thank you."

He leaned down and kissed her forehead. "I wouldn't have left you for anything in the world."

She took a few breaths and then said, "You saved my life."

The weakness in her voice shattered his heart. "I just happened to be at the right place at the right time, that's all."

She grinned. "Yeah, right." A moment passed. "You know, while I was on the bottom of that boat, I thought that was it. I thought you weren't going to find me in time and that I was going to die. But..." she closed her eyes, her brow furrowed. "As she pushed me over the boat, I heard your voice."

Overcome with emotion, he gripped her hand, bent down and lightly kissed her lips. After a moment, he said, "I can't imagine if something would've happened to you, Jolene." He pressed his forehead to hers, closed his eyes and whispered, "I want to spend the rest of my life making sure nothing ever does."

◆

Ethan woke up with a jerk as the hospital door opened. He sat up and looked at Jolene, who was still sleeping soundly.

"Good morning," the nurse whispered as she walked over to him "It's time for her medicine, and there are some officers outside wanting to talk to her."

Ethan glanced at the clock—7:30—and then looked back at the nurse. "Thank you. Let me talk to them for a second first."

The nurse smiled. "I thought you'd want to."

Ethan pushed off the cot that they called a bed, and walked out of the room. Dean and Jameson stood outside, both pale with black circles under their eyes.

"Looks like you both got as much sleep as I did."

"How is she?"

"Better. Stable. She'll go home tomorrow."

"How's her back?"

Ethan bristled. "Hundreds of stitches." He looked down. "She'll be scarred for life."

"Damn, I'm sorry. Her lungs?"

"Getting better."

"Anything we can do?"

"No, she's under good care here." He cleared his throat. "Okay, give me the rundown."

Jameson took a deep breath. "Packer's lawyers are brutal, man. Pressing us hard. But we dragged Jessica out of bed last night and had her test the blood found in Packer's apartment and sure enough, it's Chase's. So we can hold her on that for as long as this thing takes. We're also testing the knife we found on Packer for DNA, blood, anything. That'll take a day or two though. It's the same size blade that killed Debbie."

Dean nodded. "We'd like to get Jolene's interview done as soon as possible so we'll have that against her, too."

"I'm sure she'd be willing to do whatever she needs to make sure Packer gets locked up." Ethan cocked his head. "I don't understand why she would kill Chase? He was there to see Jolene, I know, but why would Packer kill him?"

"Not sure yet. We're still searching for a connection on that one." Dean shifted his weight. "So... Jolene Reeves, is it?"

Ethan nodded.

"Hmm, wonder why she would have an alias, Anna Gable?" Dean cocked his eyebrow.

Ethan paused a moment. "Jolene has a past. We've been keeping tabs on her."

Dean grinned. "I knew you knew more about her than you were leading on."

"Just a little bit."

"I think more than a little bit," he winked. "Anyway, we

need your interview, too, as soon as possible. Any way you can come down to the station?"

He glanced back at the hospital room. "Yeah, for a bit. Let me go say goodbye."

Ethan passed the nurse as he walked into the room. Jolene smiled as she saw him.

He kissed her forehead. "Coffee?"

"They're bringing me some now."

"Okay, good."

"The nurse just said I can go home tomorrow."

He smiled. "I know. Hey, Dean and Jameson are outside and want to interview you. Are you up for it?"

Fire flashed in her eyes. "You're damn right I'm up for it."

He laughed. "I thought you might be."

"Where is she?"

"Being held in jail."

"Good." She took a deep breath. "Yeah, send them in. I want to go through everything while it's so fresh in my mind."

"Okay. I've got to down to the station myself, give my interview and I've got a few things to do. I'll be back soon."

She leaned up and kissed him. "Thank you."

He smiled and gave her one more kiss on the forehead before walking out.

"She's all yours. I've got to make some calls, and then will meet you guys down at the station."

Jameson and Dead nodded. "Sounds good, see ya."

Ethan pushed through the hospital doors and inhaled the cool, crisp, fall air. Despite the horrific night, it was a beautiful morning.

As he walked to his truck, he pulled his phone from his pocket, took a deep breath, and dialed his supervisor, Mike Woodson.

"Woodson here."

"It's Ethan, how are you?"

"Hey, Ethan. How's vacation?"

"It's been interesting, to say the least."

"You better not be working, Veech."

He cleared his throat. "Well, sir, some things kind of fell into my lap."

"Go on."

Ethan laid out a detailed account of the last few days while Woodson patiently, and silently, listened. Woodson was, as always, cool, calm and collected.

"You sent the code you downloaded from Bia Wu's computer to Matt Miller for analysis, correct?"

"Yes, sir."

"Hang on." Ethan heard a few beeps. "*Miller, get in my office as soon as you can.*" Another beep. "Sorry. Alright, I'll send agents to Bia's house immediately." Ethan heard the *click, click, click,* of keys as Woodson sent an email to make arrangements for that arrest. "And you believe Packer is responsible for Senator Halstead's daughter's murder, correct?"

"Yes, sir. And for the local murders as well."

"Alright. This is our case now. I'll be on the next flight out."

"Sir?"

"Yes?"

"There's one more thing."

"I don't like one more things, Veech."

Pause. "I made a deal with Jolene Reeves, and I intend to honor it."

Ethan heard a soft groan. "What deal did you make?"

"That if she helped me by using her connections to bring down Packer, I'd have her FBI file wiped clean."

Silence.

"I wouldn't have pinned Packer down without her."

"Is there more to this story, Veech?"

He cleared his throat. "Just want to honor my promise, sir."

"And if I don't... if we can't?"

Ethan straightened behind the steering wheel and narrowed his eyes. "I'll turn in my badge upon your arrival. Sir."

CHAPTER 27

ETHAN TURNED THE empty coffee cup around in his hands as the rest of the team entered the room.

Crammed into a small conference room in the back of the police station were Ethan, Special Agent Mike Woodson, Special Agent Jake Thomas, Matt Miller, Jameson, Dean, and Chief McCord.

It had been forty-eight hours since the night Ethan had almost lost Jolene.

Woodson began the meeting. "Alright, first I want to thank Chief McCord and his team, again, for their help with this case. We've made a hell of a lot of progress in the last forty-eight hours. I wanted to quickly pull everyone together for a last minute brief." He picked up the television remote and after a few clicks, a black and white image of Chase Martinez and Slade Packer, standing in her hallway at the B&B, popped onto the screen.

"We pulled Packer's security footage. She had a hell of a security system, with hidden cameras all over. This is Chase Martinez, the day he was murdered, meeting with Packer at the B&B. This was pulled from a hidden camera in the hallway. It includes audio." He hit the play button.

"I told you never to come here, Chase. How the hell did you get in?"

"You need better locks, Barb."

"You should have known better, son."

"The bitch upstairs took my money; I'm here to get it back. And she broke my fucking wrist."

"I can't let you go up there. I don't need anything to raise eyebrows around here."

"You can't? How about if I go tell the police that I have a tip about who killed Lisa Halstead. You think that will raise some eyebrows?"

"Are you threatening me, Chase?"

"Damn straight."

Pause. *"If I go down, you go down, Chase. You did it with me. You held her feet and I held her head and we both threw her in the lake, together."*

"Just let me go get what's mine. I'll make it quick."

A long pause. *"Alright. But come downstairs with me first, I want to show you something."*

Woodson paused the screen. "We can only assume that Packer murdered Chase after they got downstairs. She was aware that her neighbor, Mrs. Chapman heard his screams so she tried to frame two of her guests instead of just dumping the body." He shuffled through a stack of papers and continued. "Furthermore, we've received the DNA results from the knife Packer had on her when Dean arrested her, and along with her own blood, we found traces of both Chase's and Debbie's."

Ethan leaned forward. "And the DNA found on the

envelope that was left on Senator Halstead's doorstep, fifteen years ago, was confirmed to be licked by a woman."

"Wasn't it determined that a Hispanic male delivered it?"

"That was Chase. They've worked together for years. Packer licked it."

Dean blew out a breath and leaned back. "So fifteen years ago, she kidnapped the senator's daughter for money, then killed her when the demands weren't met. She killed Chase Martinez because he threatened to rat her out, and she killed Debbie to send Ethan a message."

"Yes."

"What about the virus she and Bia were building?"

"Bia has been arrested and is being held in jail for questioning. Based on our findings thus far, we believe they were going to use it to hold the nukes ransom for a certain amount of money. It fits Packer's M.O."

The room sat silent for a moment.

"She'll be locked up for life."

"She'll probably serve several life sentences."

McCord leaned forward. "What about Jolene Reeves?"

Woodson glanced at Ethan, then back at the Chief. "What about her exactly?"

"I'm assuming the person Chase was referring to about taking his money was her. And she's been using a fake name, which raises suspicion regardless. She's obviously involved."

"We cannot confirm that Chase was referring to Miss Reeves in the video."

McCord narrowed his eyes. "Give me a break. Why did she use a fake name then? Come on, guys, she's involved."

Woodson coolly responded, "Who knows why she

changed her name? Maybe trying to get away from an unruly ex-boyfriend, I don't know. Women do crazy things and I've never claimed to understand why. I can tell you one thing for certain; we've looked into her extensively," he cut Ethan a glance, "and have concluded that she did nothing other than to assist us in taking down a serial killer."

McCord raised his eyebrows, crossed his arms over his chest, and leaned back in his chair.

Jameson spoke up to break the tension. "So what's next?"

Woodson glanced at his watch. "I've got a meeting with the DA in five minutes."

Jolene tipped her head back and looked at the sky. A million stars twinkled around the brightest full moon she'd ever seen in her life. She closed her eyes and inhaled as a cool breeze swept leaves across her feet. She made a mental note to stoke the fireplace before going to bed.

Sipping her wine, she gazed out to the field, dipped in the silver glow of the moon. She could see all the way to the far tree line, which backed up to the river.

An owl hooted in the distance.

"Hey."

A smile spread across her face as she looked over her shoulder.

"Hi."

Ethan crossed the porch and sat next to her on the swing. He was smiling, but she could see the exhaustion in his eyes.

He lightly smoothed the hair out of her face. "How's your back this evening?"

"Getting better."

He frowned.

She smiled; put her hand on his leg. "Don't worry. You've got enough to worry about. Speaking of, how did today go?"

He blew out a breath and gazed out at the field. "We've got almost everything tied up."

Her eyes widened and she leaned forward. "You do?"

"Yes. You won't ever have to worry about Slade Packer again."

She looked into his eyes and her heart started to beat faster. "Thanks to you, Ethan."

He looked down. "I was almost too late. One more minute, and you would have been gone."

She turned his face toward hers. "But that didn't happen. You saved my life."

He stared at her with such intensity that goosebumps ran over her body. "In the hospital, I told you that I would never let anything bad happen to you, ever again. I intend to keep that promise." He leaned forward and kissed her. "I love you, Jolene."

Emotions flooded her as she looked at him, the glow of the moon illuminating his perfect face. Her heart raced as the words began to bubble up. She kissed his lips, pulled away and then said, "I love you, too, Ethan."

He wrapped his arms around her, so tightly she could feel his body trembling.

Inside the house, her phone rang.

"Let me get that."

He pulled away, cocked his head.

She stood and smiled, "It's just something that I need to tie up."

She pushed through the screen door, grabbed her phone from the kitchen table, and walked down the hall.

"Hello?"

"Jolene, it's Dylan. Returning your call."

"Thanks for calling me back so soon."

"No problem, what's up?"

"The job, with Beckett Industries…"

"Yeah?"

"I'm out."

"*You're out?*"

"Yes."

But… why? It would make you a shit-load of money."

"I'm… starting over. Turning over a new leaf, so to speak."

"Oh, really? Honestly, I'm shocked."

Jolene laughed. "Me, too."

"I'm getting the vibe that it's not just no to this job, huh?"

Jolene turned and saw Ethan leaning against the doorway.

"That's right. No more jobs. Lose my number, Dylan. I won't be doing that kind of work ever again."

Jolene heard a chuckle on the other end of the phone. "I hope he's worth it, Jolene."

Her eyes met Ethan's, and she smiled. "He is."

"Good luck to you."

"You, too."

Click.

Ethan smiled as he walked down the hall. "You know, I wasn't going to ask."

Jolene wrapped her arms around his neck, reached up on her tiptoes and kissed his cheek. "I know."

"I'm proud of you."

"Thanks." She pulled away and put her hands on her hips. "I guess I'm going to have to find some honest work."

"Berry Springs has a lot to offer."

She looked around the cabin. "Well, I hope you're handy. I'm going to renovate the hell out of this place."

He laughed. "I sure like to think I'm handy. Jake is going to come by tomorrow before he leaves, to get the paperwork rolling. He and Katie were ecstatic when I told them you were going to buy it."

She inhaled, nodded. "I'm excited, too. I love it here. It's time for me to lay roots."

Ethan pulled her in for another hug. "And start a family."

Her heart swelled. "Possibly. So Woodson really is cool with you working remotely every few weeks?"

"Yep, I'll be down here with you as much as I can until I can arrange for something permanent."

She kissed his cheek. "I can't wait. Alright, let's go stoke the fire. It's supposed to be a chilly night."

As she turned, he grabbed her hand, his eyes flashing with desire. "Or, we could just go to bed. Get under the covers."

She grinned and he swept her off her feet.

As he carried her to the bedroom, she nestled into his neck, which had become her favorite place, and whispered. "I love you, Ethan."

If you enjoyed THE LAKE, check out the sneak peek below of the next book in the series!

THE STORM
BERRY SPRINGS
BOOK #3

HE CLICKED THE wipers on high, leaned forward and squinted to see through the frosty windshield. With each pathetic swipe, the wipers squealed and streaked, reminding him that he had the oldest damn patrol car in the department.

Dean gripped the steering wheel, his knuckles white, and his fingertips stiff from the cold. Where the hell had fall gone? According to the weatherman, Berry Springs had broken a record for the earliest ice of the season. Well, yeehaw.

He glanced down at the heater that was on full blast, but seemed to be doing nothing other than push the cool air around.

The night was pitch-black and cold as shit.

Hell of a time to be responding to a trespassing call.

Pellets of ice reflected like diamonds through the headlight beams, which were doing their best to illuminate the hairpin turns of the rugged Ozark Mountains.

To the left, a jagged cliff, and to the right, a steep ravine, with a hundred-foot drop.

Hell of a road to be speckled in black ice.

He glanced at the clock—twelve-thirty in the morning.

According to dispatch, a call was received from old man Williams, thirty minutes ago, who sworn he'd seen flashlights flickering somewhere on his forty-acre property. Williams's property line backed up to a popular hunting spot, and hiking trails. The area was heavily trafficked year-round, and the million no trespassing signs that he'd put up were commonly ignored. If there was one thing Dean knew about old man Williams, it was that he didn't take kindly to strangers being on his land. Well, that and he had a gun arsenal the size of Texas. Not a good combination.

Dean glanced down at his GPS—not that he needed to, he knew the mountain roads like the back of his hand—and pressed the brakes as he navigated a particularly tight corner. The car slid on black ice just long enough to make him say a Hail Mary.

"*Son of a bitch*," he muttered under his breath.

He softly braked again, testing the pavement, and then slowly pressed the accelerator. Straight ahead was another tight turn, with a foot-and-a-half shoulder before a drop off into the ravine.

He clenched his jaw. There'd better be a whole damn marching band to arrest.

He gripped the steering wheel, slowly edged around the curve; his headlights cutting through the darkness.

He hit the brakes.

What the hell?

He squinted and leaned forward.

Thirty feet ahead of him was… something. Something in the middle of the road.

He shoved the car into park, grabbed his hat and gloves. Sleet pinged his hat as he unfolded his six-foot-four-inch body out of the car. The moment his boot hit the pavement, he slid, catching himself on the hood.

"*Dammit.*"

He exhaled, took a minute to brace himself, and then slammed the door.

His instincts piqued immediately. Something wasn't right—he could feel it in his gut.

He reached back and loosened the strap on his Glock.

He glanced around. No one.

He closed his eyes for a moment and listened, tuning into his senses. Only the tinkling sound of the ice buzzed in his ears.

With his head on a swivel, he began walking across the pavement. The headlights shone into his back, his silhouette stretching eerily across the road.

As he got closer, the lump in the road began to take shape.

Oh, shit.

His adrenaline picked up and he broke out in a jog, each step proving what he suspected to be true.

The object in the middle of the road was a body.

He hit another patch of black ice; his pulse spiked, and his boot slid directly into the pale leg.

Shit.

His eyes widened as he looked down.

Blood and ice matted the brown hair that stuck out from the man's head. His clothes were torn and speckled with dirt. His body lay mangled and distorted on the payment, with one arm above his head and the other out to his side. His leg, broken at the knee, lay at a perfect ninety-degree angle, his ankle twisted in the opposite direction.

His bloodshot eyes stared blankly at the dark sky above.

A single bullet hole dotted the center of his forehead.

ABOUT THE AUTHOR

Amanda McKinney

Amanda McKinney, author of Sexy Murder Mysteries, wrote her debut novel, LETHAL LEGACY, after walking away from her career to become a writer and stay-at-home mom. Her books include the BERRY SPRINGS SERIES, and BLACK ROSE MYSTERY SERIES. Amanda lives in Arkansas where she is busy crafting her next murder mystery.

Visit her website at www.amandamckinneyauthor.com.

76243501R00175

Made in the USA
Middletown, DE
11 June 2018